HER NEIGHBOR

HER NEIGHBOR

A NOVEL

D.A. OLIVIER

atmosphere press

Published by Atmosphere Press

Cover design by Matthew Fielder

atmospherepress.com

For My Neighbor

CHAPTER 1

March 2019

"He looks just like Daniel," a male voice said from behind.

Julienne looked at her son lying in the hospital bed. This was day three of being in the hospital. The IV antibiotics were working and her ten-year-old was finally showing signs of improvement from the meningitis that had almost gotten the best of her boy.

Right now, Hawk was just sleeping. His spiky blond hair shot up in every direction on the pillow. He was long and thin, all knees and elbows.

Julienne was tired. She wanted a shower. She wanted her own bed. Those things would wait, though. Her place was here with her son. Her daughter, Camille, was sixteen and independent.

When she looked at Camille, she saw herself: dark hair and dark eyes. Camille was never quiet, though. She had a thought, an opinion, on everything. Julienne cherished that about her daughter. In that respect, she was so grateful Camille differed from her when she was a child.

Camille had stopped by the hospital before and after

school checking on her brother and bringing her mother coffee just the way she liked it. Camille was being a good big sister.

As Julienne shifted in her chair, the comment "He looks just like Daniel," still hung in the air.

However, Julienne had learned over the years people see what they want to see.

Julienne looked over at Hawk sleeping and thought, yes, he does look like Daniel at that age with his toothy grin and hazel eyes, but she could not say that out loud.

She wished he had not said that. She wished he had just come in the room and squeezed her shoulder, maybe given her a peck on the cheek, and asked how Hawk was doing.

Julienne squeezed her eyes shut on her wishes.

Instead, her husband had crept into the room softly and stated out loud, "He looks just like Daniel."

And to that, she had no response, not a good one anyway.

Julienne's shoulders slumped forward, and she let out a sigh. Then she shifted in the plastic green hospital chair to make eye contact with her husband, Greg.

He stood there in his signature grey suit and blue tie. His light brown hair was beginning to grey ever so slightly at the temples. His light brown eyes seemed to shimmer and Julienne realized he was holding back tears.

Part of her wanted to go to him, to assure him. They had been married for almost twenty years. Her friends from work had called them aspirational at a happy hour the other day, and if the middle-class life with a house, two kids, and a dog was your dream, then yes, they were aspirational.

Another part of her could not move and that is the part of her that won. All she could do was stare back and watch Greg screw up his face trying to keep his emotions in check.

One tear escaped and Greg quickly swatted it away like it was a fly. He shrugged his shoulders and then walked out.

Julienne again thought she should go to him, but after a moment she simply turned back around in the chair and looked back at her son.

Her mind wandered back to that week at the beach, but if she let herself remember that one week, she had to remember all of it, which would consume her. Then again, sitting in the hospital she had nothing but time.

June 2008

It took Julienne a moment to realize what the sound was waking her up. It was still dark outside. She was stuck in the middle of the bed; her husband was on one side and the dog snuggled in on the other. She had to reach across their recent rescue dog towards the nightstand. Her cell phone was vibrating away. She didn't recognize the number. It was a little after five in the morning on a Sunday.

"Hello," she answered.

There was a pause and then a click. An automated message began:

This is Harris County Jail. You're receiving a collect call from–

"Daniel Hawk," the familiar voice interjected.

At the sound of Daniel's voice, Julienne sucked in her breath.

The automated message continued:

Press one to accept. Press two...

Julienne didn't hesitate. She pressed one.

"Daniel?" she questioned.

"Jules," he said barely above a whisper. "Please come get me."

"Daniel, what happened?" Julienne questioned again.

"Jules, it's a long story. Just, please," Daniel paused. "Please come get me."

"Of course. I'm on my way," Julienne responded.

There was no graceful way for her to get out of bed, so Julienne didn't even try. She swung one leg over and half hopped out of bed so as not to disturb the dog or her husband. The dog, part basset hound/part bulldog, was a permanent brown and white lump in their bed. The dog, which her daughter had named Gaston, let out a sigh as her husband, Greg, rolled over to the other side of the bed. Julienne tiptoed to their bathroom. As noiselessly as possible Julienne brushed her teeth, washed her face, and dressed in blue jeans, a T-shirt and some flip-flops. She left Greg a note on the bathroom mirror and went to go pick up her childhood best friend. When she turned the key in the ignition, Johnny Cash was singing "Hurt" on the radio:

I hurt myself today
To see if I still feel
I focus on the pain
The only thing that's real

She wondered how her friend had hurt himself this time.

While driving, Julienne thought back to that Wednesday

in October of 1983. The leaves were just beginning to change on the one oak tree in her aunt and uncle's yard. The sky was overcast, making it seem later than a typical 3 o'clock in Houston, Texas. George Strait's "Chill of an Early Fall" was coming through the speakers of the blue Ford Taurus. George sounded sad, which matched the sky and the way eight-year-old Julienne felt.

She had been to their house before, but this time it was different. This time she was here to stay.

Her aunt and uncle were chattering away in the front seat, but she wasn't listening. As they pulled into the driveway, she saw a boy standing in the middle of the front yard next door. He had his hands on his hips, and he seemed to be surveying everything and nothing all at the same time.

She let herself out of the car. Her movements were slow. The boy was in shorts and a T-shirt. She was still in her black dress from the funeral.

He ran over to her, and she stood there frozen. He stopped right in front of her and smiled. His eyes looked blue but maybe just because he had a blue shirt on that day. He was all eyes and teeth with spiky blond hair going up to the sky.

"Are you moving in? I heard a girl might be moving in over here. How old are you? I'm nine. Maybe we can play together sometime. You have a bike? I do. I love to ride my bike. I'm your neighbor."

He seemed to say it all in one breath. She could see her aunt and uncle out of the corner of her eye waiting, wondering how she would respond. She did only what she had the energy to do–she nodded her head yes. Her dark brown eyes made contact with his but said nothing.

The boy smiled again and gave her a light tap on the shoulder. Then he took off running back to his domain. He paused before he went inside the house.

"I'm Daniel," he yelled, and then he disappeared.

Julienne's old life was over. It ended at the funeral, but in her new life she at least had one friend–a skinny, toothy boy named Daniel.

The second day at her aunt and uncle's house, there was a knock at the door. Julienne opened it, and the boy named Daniel stood there. Today his shirt was green and his eyes looked green as well. To Julienne his eyes looked familiar.

"Do you have a bike? Do you want to ride bikes with me? You can ride my brother's if you want. There's no law that says a girl cannot ride a boy's bike. My dad is working outside. He will watch us, so, do you? Want to ride bikes?"

Julienne's eyes widened as she tried to keep up with his steady stream of words. When he was done, Julienne turned back to her aunt and uncle who were waiting just like yesterday to see how she would react. Today she was dressed in shorts and her long brown hair was pulled back in a ponytail. Today she was better prepared to deal with this new neighbor.

"Go, if you want to, Julienne. It is okay," said her aunt, smiling.

She turned back to the boy, and she nodded her head yes.

"Well, then," Daniel said, motioning for her to follow him.

And that is what she did. Daniel led; Julienne followed. They rode bikes up and down the street. Their street was wide and the old trees provided an arching canopy of shade over the street. Daniel led down the sidewalk and Julienne followed. People seemed to be out and about. They all waved or called to Daniel by name. He answered them back. Julienne just took it all in with her solemn eyes. When they needed a break, they had a snack of juice boxes and pretzels in his kitchen at his house. The cabinets were a light oak and the counters were a hunter-green Formica. They sat on stools at the bar. When they were done, Daniel sprayed the counters with cleaner and Julienne wiped them down.

"My dad always makes us clean up after ourselves," Daniel explained.

Julienne just nodded. And then they rode their bikes some more. This day was less overcast with the sun peeking out from behind the clouds. Daniel's dad was cutting the grass while they rode.

When they tired of riding a second time, Daniel showed her his room. It was in the front corner of the house closest to her aunt and uncle's driveway. It looked like a boy's room with typical boy stuff. The twin bed had a coverlet with a baseball motif. He had a toy box, but most of his toys appeared to be strewn across the floor. Cars and Legos created a pattern on the wooden floor. His window was open a few inches. She stared at it.

"I leave that open for the cat," Daniel explained. "Most the time, he stays outside, but at night he likes to come in and sleep."

Julienne made a face.

"You don't like cats?" Daniel asked.

She shook her head no.

"That's okay. Maybe we'll get you a dog," he offered.

She nodded yes.

Then they heard her aunt talking to his dad. It was time for her to go back. She waved bye and walked across the lawn back to their house. Daniel stood like the day before with his hands on his hips.

The next day, her aunt and uncle enrolled her in school. She was placed in Daniel's third-grade class. Their teacher was an older lady named Mrs. Hebert, who gave all the children pats on the back. Every morning Daniel would knock on the door, and they would ride their bikes the three blocks down the road to their elementary school. At school, Daniel did Julienne's talking for her. Yes, she understood the math problem. No, she wasn't hungry. Whatever Daniel answered, Julienne went along with. It was just easier that way because she didn't have the energy to talk. Then every afternoon when the school day was over, he would safely deliver her back to her aunt and uncle.

While Julienne did not particularly like cats, she always noted Daniel's cat going in and out of his bedroom window. One night about a week after moving in she could not sleep. There were lots of nights she couldn't sleep. She would toss and turn. When she did sleep, she would dream of her parents and those dreams always ended in their death. She would wake up gasping for breath. Sleep–like talking–was an obstacle for Julienne.

On this night, she decided to see if the cat knew something she did not. She let herself out of their house and walked across the lawn and the driveway to Daniel's window. She tapped on the glass.

She heard a thud, and then his face was at the window. His hair was going in all directions, but his eyes lit up when he saw her.

"Can't sleep?" he asked.

She shook her head no.

He opened the window wider. She crawled inside.

"I thought girls wore nightgowns," Daniel commented.

Julienne shrugged. Since the accident, she had been sleeping in one of her dad's old flannel shirts. It swallowed her, but it was soft and smelled faintly of Old Spice.

Daniel, on the other hand, was wearing green pajamas with monkeys on them. They reminded her of the silly song about monkeys jumping on the bed.

"Come on," he said. He took a pillow and put it at the foot of the bed.

"You sleep there," he said, pointing to the top of the bed. "I'll sleep there," he said, pointing to the foot of the bed.

They crawled in under the baseball covers. Their feet barely touched in the middle.

"You good?" Daniel asked.

Julienne nodded.

"Oh, one more thing," Daniel said and hopped out of bed. He stood next to Julienne and explained.

"I don't remember much of my mom. She left when I was three, but I do know she always did this when she tucked me in at night. It always made me feel better."

Then he leaned over, pushed back her hair, and gave Julienne a kiss on the forehead.

"Better?"

Julienne nodded. Daniel got back into bed and they fell asleep.

When she thought back on those days, the adults in her life almost always seemed like shadows. Her aunt and uncle were nice and took very good care of her, but they were not her parents. Her teacher was also very sweet, and Daniel's dad was very patient with Daniel's new friend, a dark-haired girl who never spoke.

But in her memory the only one she remembered with any clarity was Daniel. He was the only one in sharp focus. Every time she thought of those days "Somewhere with You" played in the background as her memory's soundtrack. Kenny Chesney had it right. When she had been thrust into this new life, the only person she wanted was her neighbor. She simply preferred to be somewhere with him.

When the adults figured out Julienne went over to Daniel's there was lots of talk about appropriateness and what was healthy. The pediatrician and the school counselor were consulted. Bottom line: Julienne's aunt and uncle told her not to do that again. She did not nod in affirmation or in dissent. She just continued to stare back with her dark, solemn eyes. And she did not go again for three nights, but on the fourth night she could not sleep, so she padded across the front lawn to Daniel's house. They repeated the process from before. He once again brushed her hair back and gave her a kiss on the forehead and she slept.

This led to more conversations among the adults. Once again Julienne was told no. Once again Julienne did okay for a few nights, but then a bad night would happen. Her aunt and uncle had offered their bed if she got scared or couldn't sleep, but Julienne wanted Daniel. She let herself out of their house. Daniel let her in his. Julienne slept. Eventually the adults gave up, figuring Julienne would grow out of it. Julienne knew they were rationalizing, but she did not mind. Whenever she could not go to sleep, she slept at Daniel's house.

Harris County Jail, however, was a far cry from Daniel's house when they were little. Several forms and a large amount of cash later, an officer delivered Daniel to her.

Daniel walked with his eyes down. His hair was longer than the last time she saw him. His clothes, jeans and a shirt, hung on him. She wondered what weight he was at now.

When he finally got to her, she reached up to his face, and he turned his head. The left side of his face looked like it was used as a punching bag for hours with several cuts and a shiner forming on his left eye.

The officer had her sign one more form and left them.

"Well?" she questioned.

Daniel raised his head slowly to make eye contact. He had on a blue shirt so today his eyes looked blue. They looked blue and hollow. She hugged him and felt his ribs. He did not hug her back. She held on anyway.

"Do I need to take you to a doctor?" she asked, still holding on to him.

"No," said his hoarse voice.

"Something to eat?" she asked.

"Yes," he said.

Tears were forming in the corner of her eyes, so she held on a moment longer to get them under control.

"Okay," she said, at last letting go.

She headed in the direction of his house and stopped at the first Waffle House she saw along the way. They sat in a booth. She ordered them both coffee. Without asking, she put three sugars in his, and for her–four sugars, lots of cream. Then she ordered them both the Waffle House special. The only difference was she wanted grits; Daniel wanted hash browns. This was what they always ordered. Daniel sat silent.

She waited until Daniel had eaten some of his food and was on his second cup of coffee before trying to talk to him.

"So," she started.

"Jules," he answered, shaking his head.

"Are you going to tell me what happened?"

"You wouldn't believe me," he said, almost grinning.

"Daniel, this is me. I'm familiar with all your antics," she countered.

"Okay," he said leaning back in the booth. "You asked for it."

Julienne signaled the waitress for some more coffee; she figured they would need it.

Daniel thought back to the events of Saturday night. Flashes of images appeared in his mind. There was the barstool with his name on it. He could see the green bottle of whiskey with the red coat of arms. A girl? In the bathroom? Willie Nelson's song "Whiskey River" was coming through the speakers:

I'm drowning in a whiskey river
Bathing my memory's mind in the wetness of its soul
Feeling the amber current flowin' from my mind
And warm an empty heart you left so cold
Whiskey River take my mind

He grinned because drowning in whiskey was exactly what he had in mind.

Later in the night, there were limes and salt and a different girl he did tequila shots with, but she wanted to go and he wanted to stay and drink. Dancing? On the bar? Closing time: he remembered going up to the roof. The moon was bright. The night air was cool. Tequila girl was with him. Did he? Yep, he fucked her. She was a yeller, but there was no one to hear the sound. The roof was rough; that must be why his knees hurt. Two girls in one night, the bathroom and the roof? He remembered crawling in his truck and going to sleep.

He couldn't tell Julienne any of this. He felt like he might throw up all the food he just ate. This was an all-time low even for him and while he told his best friend everything, he could not tell her this.

"You know, you don't really need to hear this," Daniel said.

"Well, the cash I just doled out says I do," Julian retorted.

Daniel shrugged. Julienne waited.

Waffle House was full of customers. Their waitress was running around nonstop. Julienne wondered what the other customers' stories were while still waiting to hear Daniel's. Above the general noise, Julienne could just make out Coldplay's "Fix You" coming from the radio, which is what she wished she could do for Daniel. She wished she could fix whatever was eating away at him. She wished she could fix him like he had fixed her all those years ago. It was their losses that had always connected them.

Julienne let her head fall and stared at her hands in her lap. Her nails were ragged, evidence of a busy life.

Daniel nudged Julian with his foot underneath the table. Julienne looked up. Daniel began.

"Bottom line, when I left the bar last night, I was too drunk to drive, so I slept in my truck. Next thing I know a cop was knocking on my window hauling me off to jail for a DUI."

"And the beating you took?" Julienne asked.

"That happened in jail. My cellmate said I couldn't sit down."

"And," Julian prodded.

"When I was done, he let me sit down," Daniel finished.

They sat in silence. The waitress left the check. Julienne put down a twenty.

"Where next?" Julian asked.

"Home," Daniel said.

Julienne nodded yes, but that's not really where she wanted to take him. She was already forming a plan. Thankfully, Daniel fell asleep five minutes into the car ride.

When Daniel woke up, he and Julienne were definitely were not at his house.

CHAPTER 2

The beach cabin had originally belonged to her grandfather, a man she never knew. Then it was passed on to her father, a man she barely knew. Her aunt and uncle had taken the life insurance money and the money from the sale of her parents' home to raise her. That money had paid for cheer camps. It had bought her a car when she turned sixteen. It helped to pay for her college. Her aunt and uncle had kept the beach cabin, though. They always referred to it as Julienne's inheritance.

The faded blue beach cabin in the west end of Galveston was not anything special, but it was hers. It had a deck with an incredible view of the ocean. When she was little, the cabin was one of the few places she felt safe, besides with Daniel. Later it had been a place for crazy weekends with friends in college. Now it was a place for family time with Greg and Camille, when she could get them there. For the next few days, it would hopefully be a respite for Daniel.

Greg was flying out to Tulsa for business this week. Camille was spending the week with Julienne's aunt and uncle. This was supposed to have been Julienne's week to herself. She had planned to sleep late and catch up on her favorite television shows. She had booked a massage at the spa, but none of that was important now. The only thing that mattered was her neighbor, Daniel.

Daniel's reaction when Julienne had woken up was an exasperated, "Jules, what the hell?"

Before she had time to explain why she had driven an hour to the beach instead of his house, he had tromped up the stairs, let himself in, and gone straight to bed.

Julienne stayed outside on the deck to call Greg. His reaction was similar.

"Julienne, what the hell do you mean you are at the beach with Daniel?"

Julienne had explained the bailout and her decision to take him to the beach. While she could not see Greg, she knew her husband was shaking his head.

"Julienne, I, well," he sputtered. "Do you really think leaving him at our beach cabin unsupervised is the best idea?"

Julienne caught herself. Greg said our beach cabin but it only felt like hers.

"Well, he won't be alone," Julienne stated. "I will be here."

"What do you mean?"

Julienne pursed her lips and said it again, "Daniel won't be alone. I will be here."

"No."

"Excuse me," Julienne countered.

"You heard me," Greg answered. "I said no."

"You are leaving for Tulsa; Camille is with my aunt and uncle. What difference does it make? I'm spending the week at the beach."

"Julienne, there is a huge difference between you spending a week at the beach and you spending a week at the beach with him."

Julienne came back with her usual response, "Greg, please, he is my..."

"Don't say it, Julienne," Greg said through gritted teeth. "I know good and well he is your childhood friend; that excuse wore thin a long time ago. Come home."

Julienne said nothing. Seconds passed.

"Fine," Greg said and hung up the phone.

Julienne started to call him back, to plead her case, to remind Greg of all Daniel had done for her, but they had already had this conversation a few times. To say Julienne being there for Daniel had caused tension between her and Greg was an understatement. Instead, she let Greg have the last word. Maybe this wasn't the best decision she had ever made, but it was done now. She was here with Daniel.

Throughout their friendship, he had always given her the best gifts, and she meant this trip to the beach to be a gift for him.

Daniel's gift-giving started the first year she was at her aunt and uncle's. Julienne's birthday was at the end of May. She had survived since October with Daniel by her side. She still had not spoken.

Daniel continued to talk for her. Her aunt and uncle took her to weekly counseling sessions where the therapist had her color pictures. Sometimes she would take the pictures with her and show them to Daniel. He would always add on to them. He colored better than her.

Julienne had shaken her head no to a party, but yes to pizza and cake and–of course–Daniel.

Julienne had wondered about presents. She figured it was her fault for not having a party. There was no one to give her any gifts. Of course, her aunt and uncle could have gotten her something but they already did so much and they did get her cake: red velvet with cream cheese frosting. Daniel had requested it, and Julienne had simply nodded in agreement.

When she and Daniel were done eating cake, Julienne assumed they would go ride bikes. That's what they usually did.

Instead, Daniel asked, "Are you ready for your present?"

Julienne was surprised by his question.

Today his eyes were grey, reflecting the grey shirt with Spiderman on the front which he swore he wore in her honor for her birthday, but she knew he wore it because Spiderman was his favorite. She had on a yellow dress her aunt had bought her. Her hair was down instead of in its usual ponytail and she held it back from her face with a matching yellow headband. She liked the yellow dress because then she could pretend she was the Disney princess Belle. Daniel said she was like Belle because they both liked to read and they both had brown hair. Julienne had smiled at the comparison.

She had reconciled herself to no gifts, but she nodded her head yes in response to Daniel's question.

"Okay," Daniel said. "I'll be right back."

Julienne went to sit on the sofa. Her aunt and uncle were putting everything away in the kitchen, but they kept glancing over at her and smiling. Julienne waited, swinging her feet back and forth since they still did not touch the floor from the sofa.

Daniel opened the front door just enough to stick his head in and declare, “Okay, Jules. Close your eyes.”

Julienne nodded in assent and shut her eyes tight. She heard the door open wider and then shut. She could hear lots of footsteps coming towards her. It was hard to sneak up on anyone with hardwood floors. Then Daniel’s voice was right beside her.

“On the count of three, open your eyes: one... two... three.”

Julienne opened her eyes and staring back at her were the biggest, saddest pair of eyes Julienne had ever seen. The sad eyes belonged to a dog, a miniature basset hound with brown and white spots and ridiculously large floppy ears.

Julienne slowly reached her hand out towards the dog’s nose. The dog sniffed her hand and then licked it. His stumpy tail began to wag. Julienne broke into a full smile that showed all of her teeth.

“He’s from all of us,” Daniel explained.

Julienne looked up to see her aunt, uncle, Daniel’s dad, Daniel’s little brother, and of course Daniel all grinning in return at her.

“But a dog was my idea,” Daniel continued. “I picked him out. Do you like him?”

Julienne nodded yes.

“His eyes reminded me of yours. You both have big, brown eyes. You both have sad eyes.”

Julienne stood up and put her left hand on Daniel’s shoulder.

“Neighbor,” Julienne said in a hoarse whisper. “Thank you.”

Daniel gave Julienne his toothiest smile.

"Jules," Daniel said. "You're welcome."

They both stood there in the living room smiling at each other until the dog nudged her with his nose.

Julienne looked down at the eager puppy. She vaguely remembered her aunt sniffing in the background, but in that memory, it is just her and her neighbor Daniel and her dog, which they named Felix. In French, Felix meant lucky and that was how she felt when Daniel gave her the dog.

While Daniel continued to sleep, Julienne took stock of the cabin and then headed to the general store for supplies. She bought food and hit the sale racks for some clothes for her and Daniel. Shirts, shorts, flip-flops, and bathing suits were necessary, plus sunscreen. She bought some fresh flowers and wine. Then she went back to books and magazines for an easy read. She found a book by Nicholas Sparks she had not read. She put notebooks in her cart for her to write as well as a sketch pad for Daniel in case he felt like drawing. Her basket was full and her credit card took a hit, but she was smiling. She always liked being at the beach.

Later at the cabin, Julienne was putting everything away. The radio was keeping her company while she started supper. Her hair was in a messy bun on top of her head. She was drizzling olive oil in a skillet while her hips swayed to the music.

Julienne was humming along to John Cougar Mellencamp's "Hurt So Good," which always reminded her of her eighteenth birthday, when she felt warm lips on the back of her neck.

Julienne jumped and arms came around her waist.

"Easy, Jules. I got you."

Julienne took a ragged breath.

"Did I scare you?"

Julienne nodded as she relaxed into Daniel's embrace and continued with the olive oil in the skillet.

His hands came to rest on her hips and he peeked over her shoulder.

"What are you cooking?"

"Shrimp," Julienne answered. "Are you hungry?"

"Very," Daniel answered. "What can I do?"

"Pour me some wine," Julienne requested, nodding her head towards the counter where a bottle was waiting with the corkscrew next to it.

"Okay," Daniel said. Before he let go and moved to the wine, he whispered in her ear, "By the way, that's still the best tattoo."

Julienne grinned, still feeling the heat from where he had kissed it. While he poured the wine, she remembered when she had gotten the permanent ink.

When Julienne had turned eighteen, she felt like being bold. Throughout high school she had been a rule follower: teachers loved her. She made good grades; she was responsible. She was the cheerleader who was also president of the honor society. She was a model student. Daniel, on the other hand, was barely graduating high school and that was with Julienne's help. He was popular with his peers but not with the faculty. More than once, a teacher had questioned her friendship with Daniel.

She had always just smiled and said, "He's my neighbor," as if that explained it all. And in Julienne's mind it did, so when she felt like being bold she sought her neighbor for help.

The moment the idea hit her she acted on it before she

had time to change her mind. Julienne walked the familiar path across the front yard and driveway to Daniel's bedroom window. She tapped lightly.

It was a Monday night, humid and hot in Houston, Texas.

Daniel opened his window. No shirt, no shoes, just jeans.

"What's up," he asked.

"I want to get a tattoo," Julienne declared.

"Okay," Daniel said. "Give me a sec."

Any other friend would have wanted to discuss Julienne's request, but not Daniel.

Julienne waited, just standing in Daniel's front yard. Daniel came out the front door, with the addition of a shirt and shoes. Today his eyes looked green, which made Julienne smile. Green eyes always reminded her of her dad.

Over his shoulder, he yelled, "Dad, I'm going out with Jules."

Then he turned to her.

"Your car or my truck?" Daniel asked.

"Truck," Julienne decided.

And they were off. Daniel drove like he knew where he was going, which made Julienne happy because she had not thought beyond making the decision to get a tattoo. They had not spoken on the ride; Julienne listened to the radio singing, "Come on baby, make it hurt so good."

Daniel pulled up to a place called The Black Pearl Tattoo Parlor. It had the appropriate pirate motif to go along with the name. It was located at the end of a strip mall in the older part of Westbury.

They both got out. Daniel walked around to her side.

Julienne stood there. Daniel put his hand at the small of her back and nudged her forward.

Inside, the walls were painted a wine red. A tatted-up female with bleached blond hair and a corset pushing up her assets sat at a sleek black receptionist desk.

"Can I help you?" she asked.

Julienne froze. Daniel stepped in.

"She's thinking about getting a tat," Daniel said. "We both are."

"Do you know what you want?" she asked, looking at Julienne.

Julienne just stood there mute.

"Jules," Daniel said softly. "You got something in mind?"

Julienne shook her head no. She felt like they were kids again.

"Nope," Daniel answered for her.

"The gallery is over there," the receptionist inclined her head to the left. "I'll go see which artists are available."

With that, the receptionist disappeared to the back, walking on six-inch platform heels, which Julienne knew for sure would probably break one of her ankles if she attempted to wear them.

Daniel and Julienne spent several minutes perusing the wall of designs. A heart? A flower? Too predictable. Nothing she saw seemed quite right and this made her begin to doubt herself.

Then Daniel said, "What about this?"

Julienne looked over at a small but ornate fleur-de-lis. It was just right for her. Her father's family was from Louisiana. Her whole name was French.

"That's it," Julienne answered.

"Where are you going to put it?" Daniel countered.

"Here," Julienne said, picking up her long, brown hair and pointing to the back of her neck.

"That's hot," Daniel said.

Julienne blushed and gave Daniel a shove.

"No, really. Some guy will love trying to get to that tattoo to plant some kisses. It will hurt to put it right there, but it's hot."

Julienne just smiled and then she remembered his use of the word we from before.

"What about you?" she asked. "Were you serious?"

Daniel grabbed her hand and walked her over to the opposite side of the wall. He pointed to a very detailed sketch of a hawk in flight with its wings spread out. The picture deserved to be framed and displayed. Julienne would have never thought to tattoo an image like that.

"Too literal?" Daniel asked.

"It's beautiful," Julienne replied. "And, no, Daniel Hawk. It's not too literal."

Julienne continued to admire the tattoo. "So, how many times have you been here before?"

Daniel smirked, "A few. The guy has been pretty patient working with me. I wasn't sure, but then you knocked on my window wanting one, too, so I knew it was time to pull the trigger."

Julienne just nodded. She thought she was being so bold doing something even Daniel hadn't thought of, but of course, he already thought of it. She just shook her head. She was glad they were doing this together.

Thirty minutes later, J Badass in a plaid flannel button-down which was missing the sleeves was working on Daniel, who was laid out without a shirt. His hawk was going on the top left-hand side of his back. It was going to take up a quarter of his torso.

Meanwhile, Mr. Mike in white tank and black leather pants was working on Julienne's neck. Her hair was all pinned up and Daniel was right. It hurt like hell. However, her ordeal was over much sooner than Daniel's was.

When they got ready to leave, Julienne started to dig in her purse for her money.

"Don't worry," Daniel interjected. "I got it. Consider it your birthday present."

Julienne just smiled.

Later, they celebrated with beer Daniel bought with his fake ID.

Once again, Julienne put her hand on Daniel's shoulder and said, "Neighbor, thank you."

Now here they were, no longer young and at least for Julienne no longer bold–although maybe this trip to the beach might be classified as crazy.

You don't have to be so exciting
Just trying to give myself a little bit of fun, yeah
You always look so inviting

Now Daniel sang along as he poured her some wine while she sautéed the shrimp in olive oil and garlic. She planned to serve it over linguine. The salad was already tossed and on the table.

"This is nice, Jules," Daniel commented as he watched Julienne continue to cook. "Not really like you, but I like a little impromptu trip."

Julienne put the pasta in the strainer and arched an eyebrow at Daniel over the steam that was rising from the hot water as it poured into the sink.

"What?" Daniel asked. "I'm complimenting you. I always like some fun in the sun."

Julienne just shook her head as she moved the pasta to a serving dish and coated it with butter and some fresh parmesan.

She moved everything to the table and nodded for Daniel to join her.

Daniel fixed his plate. Julienne waited until his mouth was full to comment on his fun in the sun statement.

"Daniel, you know this trip to the beach isn't just for fun, right?"

Daniel narrowed his eyes at her as he finished chewing his bite of shrimp and pasta. He took a sip of water.

"What do you mean, Jules? A few days at the beach–I love it."

"No," Julienne answered back. "You don't love it. Don't act all casual about me hijacking you to the beach. I am giving up my week for you."

Daniel stared at her and then took another bite of food. Julienne took a sip of wine and waited.

"Don't act like a martyr, Jules. You aren't giving up anything. You are dying for something different than that boring mundane life you lead and I'm happy to tag along, but don't act like the beach is for me; it's for you."

"Not hardly," Julienne answered back. She could feel the heat rising up her neck to her cheeks. She could not believe how flippant he was being, acting like his night in jail had not happened, like her bringing him to the beach was about her and not him.

"Daniel, the only reason we are here is for you. My week was planned completely different, but after seeing you like that at the jail, the only thing I could think to do was to bring you here to give you a few days to get–"

Daniel pushed away from the table and stood up. He was leaning over the table and glaring at her.

"To get what, Jules?" he asked. "What do I need to get?"

Julienne leaned back in her chair and maintained eye contact.

"To get right," she answered. "I brought you here to get better, to get right."

"I need to get right?" Daniel asked as he poked himself in the chest. He started towards the sliding doors and then turned back around.

"I need to get right, according to you, but Jules, you need to get right, too. You may not have been thrown in jail last night, but then again there are different forms of jail. Your life isn't any more right than mine is."

With that, Daniel went out to the deck. In another moment she could see the orange glow of his cigarette. He was smoking. She was sitting by herself at the table and decided to go ahead and eat. She took another sip of wine and thought back to another trip that had definitely gone better than this one had so far.

When Julienne turned twenty-one, she found herself sitting at a bar in the heart of the French Quarter in New Orleans. She and Daniel had paused long enough at their hotel to check in and drop off their bags. The rest of the afternoon had been spent exploring the Quarter.

A lady with a flower in her hair and a low, sultry voice was singing the blues to the patrons of their current bar. The air was sticky but not that different from the humidity of Houston. The smells were different, though. In New

Orleans you breathed in the Quarter: you breathed the coast along with the alcohol and tabasco all rolled together into one smell.

Daniel motioned to the bartender for another whiskey. Julienne was still sipping on her beer, a local favorite made with sugarcane. An older man sat down on the other side of Julienne. When the bartender brought Daniel's drink, the gentleman asked for a beer and a shot of tequila.

"Tequila, huh?" Julienne asked.

The man nodded his head.

"Who did the breaking?" Julienne asked.

"Excuse me," the man said, giving her a sideways look.

Julienne and Daniel were in New Orleans to celebrate her birthday. The man sitting next to them looked somewhere around forty. His hair was light brown with gold streaks. His face was tan. His hands were big and calloused. Julienne thought he could go straight to any casting call wanting a ruggedly handsome American man.

Julienne persisted in the conversation with the stranger.

"Tequila usually means heartbreak. You break hers or vice versa?" Julienne questioned.

The man just stared at her.

"Jules," Daniel said almost as an admonishment. He touched her knee, wanting her to face him and not the guy drinking the tequila.

Julienne didn't budge. The bartender put the beer and the tequila down in front of the man. He took the shot without hesitation. Then he turned to face Julienne.

"She did," he said with no emotion.

"How?" Julienne asked.

"I caught her sleeping with my best friend," he replied

again, matter-of-factly.

"When?" Julienne asked.

"This morning," he answered, maintaining eye contact.

"No shit?" Julienne asked.

"No shit," the man answered.

Julienne looked at the bartender.

"Tequila shots for all three of us."

The bartender just nodded.

"I'm Julienne. This is Daniel. And whatever her name is, she didn't deserve you."

The man just nodded. The bartender served their shots. And that was the beginning of the end.

They found out his name was John. He had been married for ten years. He wanted kids; she didn't. He loved her; apparently, she loved his best friend.

Julienne had the band play "Matilda," and she took John for a spin out on the dance floor. He surprised her with a few spins and a dip at the end. He almost smiled when he told her thank you for the dance. Daniel just shook his head and ordered more drinks.

Later the band played "Let It Be Me." Without a word, Daniel took her hand and guided her out to the dance floor. They both smiled without acknowledging the importance of that song. No matter what the song, Julienne liked to slow dance with Daniel. With heels on, her head reached his shoulder. He would hold her close right at the small of her back and sing softly into her ear. She always felt safe dancing with him.

When they came off the dance floor, John asked how long they had been together.

Julienne just laughed, but Daniel responded, "About

twelve years."

John paused then said, "Really?"

Julienne chimed in, "Yep, really."

John just shrugged and ordered another round for all three of them.

When the bar shut down, they put John in a cab and walked back to their hotel. Along the way they came across a muffuletta cart.

Julienne insisted, so Daniel bought them one to split.

With a mouthful of sandwich and cheese hanging off her chin, Julienne declared, "This is the best birthday ever."

Daniel took a napkin and wiped away the cheese. Then he pulled her in tight and said, "I'm glad, Jules, I'm glad."

Julienne grabbed his hand and they finished the walk back to their hotel.

The next morning over Bloody Marys, Julienne rehashed the night before.

"Poor John," she declared.

"Yea," Daniel commented. "That's rough."

"I can't imagine. Loving someone and calling them yours for ten years, then that," Julienne trailed off.

Daniel continued to drink, letting Julienne think out loud.

"People suck sometimes."

Daniel nodded in agreement.

"I guess loss comes in many forms," Julienne continued. Daniel squeezed her hand. Julienne took a big sip. They sat in silence.

When their food arrived, Julienne did not immediately dig in. Daniel kicked her shin under the table.

Julienne looked up. Her eyes were super moist. There

were dark circles underneath them from lack of sleep. Daniel knew she was tired and hungover and maybe this added to her being near tears over a stranger they just met at a bar the night before.

"Jules," Daniel said softly. "Don't be sad."

"What if I lost you?"

Daniel shook his head. "Never happen."

"But it could. What if after all these years of calling you my neighbor, you weren't anymore."

A tear trickled down her face. She knew she was being silly but she couldn't help it.

"Here," Daniel said, handing her his napkin.

Julienne wiped the tear away and then blew her nose. She took another sip of her Bloody Mary and then attempted a smile.

Daniel just laughed. Her face was red and blotchy from the tears and the runny nose and there she was giving her best smile.

"What?" Julienne said, picking up her fork, ready to rally and to eat.

"You," Daniel said continue to chuckle. "You are a mess, a beautiful mess," he said shaking his head. "I could paint you this way."

Julienne, with a mouthful of pancake, responded, "Yeah, right."

Then they both proceeded to devour their breakfast.

That night Daniel took her out to a fancy restaurant for her birthday dinner. He was ready first and headed to the hotel bar. Julienne finished curling her hair which she knew would not stay in the NOLA humidity, but she attempted the curls anyway. Then she put on her dress-red with spaghetti straps. It hit just above the knee. A spritz of perfume and she was ready.

When she walked into the hotel bar, she did not see Daniel right away. She stood for a moment surveying the room. The bartender gestured to someone and then Daniel turned around.

He had on a light blue button-down shirt with navy slacks. His hair was combed back. His eyes sparkled, reflecting the blue he wore.

Julienne walked towards him and Daniel's smile grew bigger. She stopped in front of him and he continued to smile.

"What?" Julienne asked, shifting her weight back and forth in the heels she had on that night.

Daniel grabbed her wrist and leaned in to whisper in her ear, "I like you in red. You look beautiful."

Julienne felt herself blush. Daniel motioned for her to sit. The bartender poured her a glass of champagne.

"What is this for?" Julienne asked.

"Your birthday, silly," Daniel answered. "Cheers," Daniel said and held up his glass.

Julienne clinked glasses with him and enjoyed the bubbles as they went down.

"Okay, Jules, cover your eyes," Daniel ordered.

This reminded Julienne of when they were kids. She was not big on surprises, but this was Daniel so she obeyed.

A moment passed.

Then Daniel said, "Open."

Julienne opened her eyes to a Tiffany blue jewelry box with a white bow.

Julienne's eyes sent him a questioning look.

Julienne shook her head.

"You weren't supposed to get me a gift," she declared. "This trip is my gift."

"Jules," Daniel said her name emphatically. "Open the gift."

Julienne slid off the bow. Inside the box was a sterling silver J on a delicate silver chain.

Julienne's hand went to her mouth.

"Well," Daniel asked.

Julienne smiled.

"Put it on," Daniel suggested.

Julienned turned around. The chain felt cold on her neck as Daniel slipped the necklace on. Julienne lifted her hair for Daniel to clasp the necklace and his breath was warm on her neck.

"Done," Daniel exclaimed.

Julienne let her hair fall back down and turned to the mirror behind the bar. The "J" necklace was just the right touch to go with the dress. Her left hand reached up to touch the letter. Then she turned to Daniel.

"Do you like it?" Daniel asked.

Julienne gave him a hug and whispered, "I love it. Thank you, neighbor."

She still wore her "J" necklace every day, but not all gifts lasted.

Julienne shook her head at herself as she ate the last of the food on her plate. Daniel was sitting in one of the red chairs just staring out at the beach. She grabbed his water and plate of food and went outside to join him.

She sat down beside him and without saying a word placed his food and water on the wide arm of the deck chair. Julienne tucked her feet up underneath her and looked out at the waves. Daniel grabbed the plate and began eating. The constant crashing of the Galveston waves was the only noise.

"Thank you," Daniel said when he was done eating.

"You're welcome," Julienne answered.

"So, we are really here for me?" Daniel asked, reaching for her hand.

Julienne let him take it and just nodded yes.

"Okay," Daniel said as he held onto her hand and turned his attention back to the waves. He leaned his head back and closed his eyes.

"Daniel?" She said his name as a question.

"Yes," he answered with his eyes still closed.

"What's wrong with my life?" she said in a quiet voice. She hated the way the question came out because she sounded like a little girl all over again but she also had to ask. It was the first time Daniel had ever expressed a negative opinion over the life she was leading.

Daniel just squeezed her hand.

"Oh, Jules," Daniel said, almost a sigh. "That is a conversation for another time. Tonight, I will accept the spotlight. I'm the one who needs to get right."

"Yes, but," Julienne began.

Daniel opened his eyes and turned his head to look at her.

"Just don't pity me," he pleaded. "I want a lot from you, Julienne, but I never want your pity."

It was the use of her actual name which quieted her. He never used her first name; he always used the childhood nickname of Jules.

She returned his gaze and nodded her head. They could talk about her another time. They just sat holding hands and watching the sunset, listening to the waves crash, and she hoped in the end, this gift of the beach would be good enough for Daniel.

Gifts always made her think of Felix, the dog with sad eyes like hers.

Julienne still remembered sitting in the cubicle at the vet's office. It was February of 1995. Her dog's head was in her lap. She was stroking his head. He was old and in pain; his eyes were even sadder than usual. His tail did not wag at all. Julienne still could not wrap her mind around the news the vet had delivered.

One of the techs came in asking, "Are you ready?"

Julienne just shook her head no.

"Okay, take your time," the tech started to leave the room then turned and asked, "Is there anyone you want to call?"

Julienne shook her head no. She wanted to say I already did or he'll be here any minute, but all she could do was shake her head.

Instead, she continued to sit with her dog, Felix. Dogs didn't live forever and Julienne felt silly for not being better prepared for this.

Sometime later, the door opened. Standing in the doorway was Daniel.

His hair was combed with a deep part on the side. He had paint on his shirt so she knew he must have been working on a project. His eyes made contact with hers and immediately sobs escaped from her which shook her whole body. Daniel knelt down and hugged both of them.

Later, in the parking lot Julienne reverted back to quiet. Her aunt and uncle had called her that morning and she had driven straight in to be with Felix. She hadn't eaten. She was behind on sleep. She wanted to go right back to Sam Houston University and pretend her dog hadn't just died. The sky was clear and the sun was shining and no one–not even Daniel–in this moment understood how she felt. What she wanted most was not to feel.

Daniel kept chattering away:

What did she want to eat?

Had she seen her aunt and uncle yet?

How long was she staying?

Did her professors know why she was missing?

"Shut up," Julienne said in a hoarse whisper.

Daniel kept talking.

"Shut up," Julienne said, louder this time.

"What?" Daniel asked.

"I said shut up," Julienne repeated, stomping her foot. "Just shut up."

"Jules," Daniel said, his eyes pleading. She had never hollered at him before.

"This is all your fault," Julienne shouted.

A lady walking out with her cat in a crate looked at them quizzically. Daniel smiled. The lady kept walking. Julienne turned and walked away as well.

Daniel grabbed her by the wrist. She swung back around and hit him in the shoulder. Then she pushed him away with both hands as hard as she could. Daniel just stood there with his arms down by his side.

"This is all...your...fault," she said again, giving volume to each word.

Daniel continued to stand there and let her vent. Mascara was running down her face. Her nose was red. Her eyes were already puffy from the crying. Daniel wanted to hug her, but he held back.

Eleven years ago, Julienne's parents had died. Since

then, she had not had to deal with death. Not until now, not until the dog Daniel had given her on her ninth birthday had to be put down.

Julienne's face was twisted up in so much pain, and Daniel–who had always instinctively known how to help his friend–was at a loss.

Julienne gulped in a breath and willed herself to quit crying. She wiped her face with her hand, which only served to smear her mascara further. She took one more breath and then looked at Daniel, holding his eye contact.

Back to a whisper, Julienne declared, "I hate everything about this day."

Then she ran to her car and left.

Daniel just stood in the parking lot processing what had just happened until his phone chirping broke his trance. Caller ID showed it was Julienne's aunt and uncle. He answered the call as he walked to his truck. He knew they were worried; so was he.

That night around midnight, Daniel heard a knock on his apartment door. Standing on his doorstep was Julienne. Her face had been washed clean but still showed the effects of crying.

He opened the door wider. She walked under his arm straight to his bedroom. She took off her shoes, put her keys and phone on the nightstand, and crawled into bed. Daniel turned off the light and got in on the other side. She rolled over to put her head on his shoulder. He held her tight. This was the first time they slept like a normal couple and not like the way they had as kids. Soon Daniel felt her body relax and knew she was asleep, but he continued to hold on anyway.

The next morning Julienne drove back to Sam Houston

University. They never spoke of the dog Felix again.

As Julienne sat there with Daniel on the deck on their first night at the beach, she figured his night in jail would go in the vault as well. After they dealt with this incident, it would never be spoken of again. That's what they did with hurtful memories. They locked them away.

Julienne looked over at her friend, who had fallen asleep. His face was still a swollen mess of pink, purple, and red. One lock of hair fell over his eyes and his steady breathing calmed her reaction to his face. She eased her hand from his. She went inside to retrieve a blanket and took it back out to cover him since it was getting cooler with the sun down. Julienne picked up the remnants of their meal and then crawled into bed with the paperback she had bought earlier in the day. After three pages, she could barely keep her eyes open. Her day had started early and had been draining. She turned off the lamp and went to sleep. Sometime during the night, she felt Daniel get into bed with his head at the opposite end. His hand found her ankle and they both went back to sleep.

CHAPTER 3

The next morning Julienne woke up to the sun shining through the sliding doors in the master bedroom, which led out to the deck. She yawned and stretched and sat up to check on Daniel. He was lying on his back with one hand behind his head. His face was a little less swollen. Every time she looked at him, she was both sad and mad. The cut on his lip reminded her of the one time she received a busted lip at the hands of someone else. She had not thought of that night in a long time.

Seventeen-year-old Julienne had started her car, not sure of where she was going. She just knew she couldn't stay at Stephen F. Austin with her jerk of a boyfriend, now ex-boyfriend. She flipped through the radio channels and landed on the beginnings of a Van Morrison song. The guitar was strumming a slow syncopated beat and then he began to sing:

We were born before the wind
Also younger than the sun

Ere the bonnie boat was won as we sailed into the mystic

Julienne smiled even though it hurt with the cut on her lip. She knew exactly where she was going and she hoped he would be there.

It was midnight when she pulled into the duck camp. The sky was a dark blue with just a sprinkling of stars like rhinestones decorating the night. There was a slight chill in the air and Julienne was cold since she had dressed to impress and not for the weather. The halter top left her shoulders bare and she moved her shoulders as if to shrug off the cold.

She sighed in relief to see his truck parked there. He had said he was coming up this weekend, but with her luck he could've bailed.

She tapped lightly on the door. And waited. The cabin was old and worn. It had been in Daniel's family for three generations. One minute went by and she tried again, louder this time. She heard movement from within.

Daniel opened the door just a few inches. His hair was all over the place. He had on no shirt, no shoes, just jeans that hung low on his hips.

He took one look at her and opened the door wider, saying, "Jules, Jesus Christ. What happened?"

Julienne had thought about what had happened that night the whole way up there. He had slapped her hard that night, which was the cause of the split lip. He had pushed her before–even left a bruise one time from gripping too hard–but her boyfriend had never hit her until tonight.

She had tasted the blood in her mouth, but she held

her ground, looked at him with shoulders squared, and spat out the words, “Fuck you.”

His response was to push her, harder than she expected, and she went flying. She tried to catch herself, but her head caught the corner of his nightstand on the way down. She stayed on all fours and let the impact sink in. She was a senior in high school. Last year when they had been in school together, they had been the “it” couple: her a cheerleader, him a football star. But this year he was in college. He was different, and this relationship was definitely not working. Her high school had a Friday open with no game and she thought she would surprise him by driving up, but this was not what she had in mind.

It felt like a herd of elephants was stampeding inside her head. She took a deep breath and then another.

“God dammit, Julienne,” he said. “Get up,” he continued.

She did not move. She was not sure she could. Instead, she slowly began to crawl around on the floor looking for her keys and her purse.

“Quit being so dramatic,” he said. He was pacing now.

She found her things and then she used the bed to help push herself up. She felt a trickle of blood run down the side of her face from where she hit the nightstand.

“It’s just sex,” he spouted. “Why can’t we have sex?”

Julienne headed for the door–taking slow steps, but heading out just the same.

“If you leave now,” he said emphatically, “We’re through.”

She kept walking. She got two steps outside his door and threw up in the hallway. No way was she coming to school here next year, she thought to herself. All of this flashed through her mind as Daniel waited for an answer, but all she could do was shake her head and walk past him into the cabin. The cabin was one large room with a kitchen and eating area on one side and beds and sofas on the other. In the back was a door that led to a bathroom on the right and a utility room on the left.

Daniel just shook his head and closed the door. Julienne took a hot shower to get all the blood out of her hair. The tiles in the shower were a faded yellow and the shower curtain had ducks on it, which as a child always made her smile when they brought her up to the camp. When she got out of the shower, he had left her some of his clothes to put on to replace the halter top and too short skirt. She walked out in one of his shirts, some boxers, and her wet hair wrapped in a towel.

Daniel motioned at her to get in bed. He had gotten out extra blankets, knowing Julienne was always cold. The old brass bed had lost most of its luster but was still sturdy. Julienne had always claimed it as hers ever since the first time she visited the camp. She sat Indian-style on the bed and leaned against the pillows.

Then Daniel went at her cuts with peroxide and ointment. She winced; he kept going. For being a good patient, Daniel rewarded her with a beer. She drank her beer in bed under the covers, leaning against the headboard. He sat on top of the covers at the other end.

"Do you want to talk about it?" Daniel asked.

Julienne knew he would have lots of questions, but she shook her head no.

"You know I'm going to kill him, right?" he added.

"Daniel, no," she said grabbing his hand. "He's not worth it."

He stared at her. His eyes were light brown tonight. She stared back, not wavering. Her bottom lip was swollen and she had a gash in the upper left side of her forehead.

"But if he would do this," Daniel began again.

"I know," she whispered back.

"And you aren't going to school there next year. We'll find somewhere else for you to go," he continued.

"I know," she whispered again.

"And if I ever see him," Daniel rattled on.

Julienne squeezed his hand and said, "Daniel, I know."

He stared at her again. She attempted a smile but it came out lopsided due to the cut lip.

"What pissed him off this time?" Daniel asked.

She looked down and said to the covers she was staring at, "I wouldn't have sex with him."

With no pause at all Daniel answered, "Well, of course not. Why would you have sex with a jackass like that?"

Julienne shrugged. "He's tired of waiting. We've been together for a year now. He doesn't understand me holding on to my virginity," she said, making quote marks with her hand when she said the word "virginity."

"He's an idiot," Daniel snorted. "You'll have sex when you are ready, when it's right, when it's special."

Julienne set her now empty beer down on the nightstand.

"Is that what you did?" Julienne asked, already knowing the answer. "Was it so special with Madison in the back seat of her car?"

Daniel grinned.

Julienne continued on teasing.

"Fifteen years old, making it with a senior. Your reputation grew to epic proportions. Meanwhile, three years later I'm the last virgin of our senior class."

Daniel took the last swig of his beer and replied, "First of all, you are not the last virgin. Second, Madison was a thing, not a relationship. And yea, at the time it was pretty special."

They both laughed.

"Seriously, Jules," Daniel went on, "any guy in a relationship with you would be lucky and they should wait as long as you want because being with you is special."

Julienne took the towel down from her hair and proceeded to towel dry the dampness that was still present.

"I don't know," she replied. "Sometimes I just think I want to get it over with."

"Well, in that case," Daniel countered, "why didn't you just have sex with him tonight?"

Julienne thought about it for a moment and with a grin replied, "Well, because he's a jackass."

"Exactly," Daniel said with a wink. Then he reached over to give her a kiss on the forehead. She turned off the lamp and they went to sleep just like when they were kids.

And now, here they were at the beach acting like they were kids all over again, but they weren't. Julienne for the second morning in a row slipped out of bed as noiselessly as possible so as not to wake the other person in the bed. In the bathroom she put on some shorts and her tennis shoes. She pulled her hair up and headed to the kitchen. She started the coffee and then grabbed her sunglasses on her way out.

Julienne made her way to the beach. Her first thought was she would go for a run, but now she was thinking maybe a walk instead. The wind smelled of salt and seaweed. No one else was on the beach at this time of the morning and the quiet called for a slow pace. Julienne started walking and let her thoughts wander.

Julienne remembered another night she had shown up at Daniel's out of the blue. It was a random night in college when she had been out with the girls in downtown Houston.

The cab had pulled up to Daniel's house. No lights were on inside. She handed the driver a twenty-dollar bill and got out. The night air had felt good on her face.

Julienne was tipsy: a steady stream of drinks at dinner, the concert, and the bar afterwards would do that to you. When both of her girlfriends had abandoned her for hook-ups at the bar, Julienne had found herself with no way home.

But then again, she had not felt like going home just yet, so instead she showed up at Daniel's house at two a.m. instead.

Pausing on the sidewalk, she texted him. Then she looked up at the sky. The band Blue October was still in her head. She began to hum along to their song "Sway" as she waited for Daniel's response. "Houston, dance with me," she heard the lead singer Justin say in her mind as she continued to gaze at the night sky.

Her phone buzzed: Back door is open.

Julienne smiled and walked up the driveway. She let herself in and tried not to make too much noise. Daniel's roommate had the master bedroom downstairs and Daniel had a loft apartment upstairs.

Julienne was sporting thigh-high, high-heeled boots that night. Julienne felt fairly tall, but also very loud as her heels clicked on the wooden floor. When she got to the bottom of the stairs, Daniel opened his door from above.

He stood at the top of the stairs. The light from his bedside lamp cast a glow that lit him from behind. As usual, he had no shoes and no shirt. His jeans were low on his hips and Julienne could see that cut that guys get right there where their abs and their hip bone meet. His hair was rumpled and his eyes looked heavy, like he had been sleeping.

Daniel put his arms overhead and grabbed the door frame leaning forward slightly.

Julienne continued up the stairs and thought: Damn, he's sexy.

The thought startled her and she shook her head in response. Daniel grinned as she reached the top of the stairs. He moved to the side to let her in, stating:

"Two questions."

Julienne put her clutch down on his dresser and waited.

"Were you dancing on my sidewalk?"

Julienne smiled. Her lips still had remnants of the red lipstick she had applied at the beginning of the night. "More like swaying," she answered in response.

"Okay," Daniel said, still grinning. "Second question: what are you wearing?"

Julienne did a twirl to show off her thigh-high boots and sequin shorts topped with a blazer and a hint of a lacy black bra underneath.

When she finished her twirl, she declared, "I call it hooker chic. Sarah insisted we get dressed up tonight."

Daniel continued to stare at her with his hands on his hips. His eyes moved down and back up again.

"Damn, Jules, you look hot."

"Really?" she questioned. Daniel would tell her when she looked pretty-usually at moments when she felt the least pretty-but he had never told her she looked hot before.

"Yea," he replied. "Smoking hot."

"So, what you are saying is," Julienne said as she stepped closer to Daniel, "if you didn't already know me and you saw me tonight..."

Daniel interjected, "I totally would have hit on you."

He gave her a good game pat on her sequined butt as he headed for the sofa.

"Would you paint me like this?" Julienne smirked.

Daniel stared up at her from the sofa. He looked up and down her body once more. Julienne waited, licking her lips.

Daniel shook his head no.

"Really," Julienne questioned again. "Why not?"

"I just wouldn't," Daniel said, dismissing the question. He patted the space on the sofa beside him. "Now, come sit down."

"No," Julienne said. "You come stand up."

"You're drunk," Daniel stated.

"Maybe," Julienne acquiesced as she held out her hand.

"Yes," Daniel said, standing up and taking her hand. "What are we doing, Jules?"

She put her arms around his neck and answered, "Dancing."

Daniel pulled her in, saying, "But there's no music."

"So," Julienne retorted. Daniel's body felt warm and she leaned into him. She rested her head on his shoulder and they began to sway.

"So, the concert was good," Daniel said, making small

talk as they moved back and forth.

Julienne looked up. She put a finger to his lips.

"Don't talk," she ordered. "Just dance."

Julienne put her head back on his shoulder. Daniel complied and remained silent. They continued to move. She could almost fall asleep.

The next thing Julienne knew, she was up in the air. Daniel had scooped her up and was carrying her to the bed. He laid her down on the mattress. She held her breath in anticipation. Then he took off each boot, sliding them down and pulling them off. Next, he slid off her sequin shorts. Underneath was a pair of black lacy underwear which matched the bra.

Julienne wasn't sure what was happening. She waited to see what Daniel would do next.

Daniel unbuttoned her blazer and lifted her up just enough to slide it off. Then he disappeared. Julienne took a breath.

Julienne was just lying there on top of Daniel's bed in her bra and panties. She felt exposed and unsure, which was intensified by the fact that those feelings were with Daniel, the one person she always felt safe with no matter what.

Daniel returned with a T-shirt. He slipped it over her head. She was left to push her arms through the sleeves. Then he disappeared again. Julienne took another breath. This time he returned with a bottle of water and two aspirin. He handed the pills to her without saying a word. She took the pills and drank the water. She felt like a little girl.

Daniel put the bottle on the table next to the bed. Then he pulled up the covers and gave her the customary kiss on the forehead. He turned the lamp off. Then he walked away.

The room was dark at this point except for the soft glow emanating from the television. Daniel had returned to the sofa and was watching whatever he had on before she got there.

Julienne exhaled. She was not sure if she was relieved or disappointed. She rolled over to her side and went to sleep, unsure of what just happened–or in this case, didn't happen.

She woke up the next morning greeted by the sunlight streaming in through the window. Daniel was beside her on top of the covers. Julienne yawned and stretched. Then she tried to peer over him to see the clock on his side of the bed.

"Well, hello there, sunshine," Daniel said.

Julienne looked away from the clock and down at him. His grey shirt was too big for her and hanging off of one shoulder. Her hair was a tangled mess falling into her face. She gave him a half-smile that did not show her teeth because she desperately needed to brush them.

Daniel pushed her hair out of the right side of her face and grinned. In the morning light, his eyes looked green, her favorite.

"Now this is the Jules I would paint," he declared.

Julienne shook her head no and laid back down on the pillow. Daniel propped himself up on his side. Julienne shook her head no, again.

"Oh yea, with the morning light streaming in like this. You in my shirt in my bed all rumpled. Oh yea, I would paint this."

Julienne had no reply, so she continued to lie there and

said nothing.

Daniel laughed and patted her head.

"Someone needs coffee," he said as he got out of bed.

Julienne nodded in agreement and just like that they continued on in the regular cadence of their friendship.

Julienne smiled at the memory. She had walked beyond the point of recognizing the cabins, so she decided to turn around and walk back. She slipped off her shoes and let her feet sink into the warm sand. Putting her shoes in one hand, she just stood for a moment breathing in the beach air, holding her face up to the sun, soaking in the rays and the memories.

CHAPTER 4

Back at the cabin, Daniel was busy making scrambled eggs and toast. Julienne fixed her coffee and watched him work.

When Julienne thought of Daniel, she always went back to her first image of Daniel standing in his yard. He was her neighbor Daniel, but not everyone saw Daniel the same way she did.

As sweet as Daniel was in elementary school when Julienne first met him, he became the exact opposite in middle school. Of the boys in their class, Daniel grew first, making him the biggest and the meanest. Daniel in middle school was quick to push and even throw a punch usually for seemingly no reason other than the other person was just in his presence. More than once, Daniel was suspended. Daniel's dad would just shake his head and punish him. Teachers described him as insolent and constantly angry.

The only classes Daniel did well in were woodshop and art. No matter how sullen Daniel was, Julienne remained his friend; consequently, Daniel was never angry with her.

No one seemed to know what made Daniel so mad, but Julienne did. They never talked about it, but she knew Daniel's anger stemmed from his mother. He knew she knew and that was enough. Julienne understood.

Julienne remembered the day she had found him in the library staring at a computer screen. His face was red. Looking over his shoulder, she saw he was looking up arrest records. When she touched his shoulder, he just stared at her, then he got up and left. Julienne took his place. She saw his mother's name.

When Daniel was little, he had always imagined his mother would come back. Julienne wondered if that was another reason for the open window. The cat came through it, Julienne came through it; maybe he hoped one day his mother would come through it as well.

Julienne was able to piece together a history of addiction, rehab, and arrests that were usually drug-related. She figured that was the reason Daniel's dad had full custody of the boys and her inability to stay clean was the reason she had no visitation. She often wondered how that must feel for a parent to choose drugs over their child. Her parents had died in a wreck. They had not chosen to leave her; however, to a twelve-year-old Daniel who'd discovered facts about his mother he had never known, he must have felt like his mother had made a choice.

Julienne understood the original source of his anger; therefore, Julienne was the only person Daniel was never angry with in those years. Daniel was not angry now; in this moment he was humming while cooking. Every now and then he would look up to make sure Julienne was still there. As she watched him cook, she still saw glimpses of that little boy who sought her out, who protected her, but needed her approval as well.

"Jules, put on some music," Daniel requested, interrupting her thoughts.

Julienne turned on the radio that had been here for as long as she could remember. She turned the dials until a classic country station came through clear.

"You're the reason God made Oklahoma," was twanging through the speakers. Daniel caught her around the waist and two-stepped her to the cabinet, indicating the dishes. Julienne grabbed plates and forks and hummed along as well. She was glad to see Daniel perk up a little, but the song with its Oklahoma reference made her think of her husband.

Greg was very tactful the first time he officially met Daniel. Greg had been her date to Daniel's wedding but the two men had yet to sit down and speak. They were supposed to meet up with Daniel and his wife, Tara, for drinks, but Tara bailed at the last minute. This meant Julienne was out with the two men in her life.

Daniel told old stories of their childhood. Greg told new ones from their time in graduate school where their paths had first crossed.

Greg was from Oklahoma. He liked barbeque and baseball. He had an MBA from the University of Tulsa and lived in a world of spreadsheets.

Daniel liked gumbo and football. His degree was from the Houston Art Institute. He lived in the world of paint and clay.

Julienne spent the evening sipping on captain and coke while watching the two men posture. For them, it was sport. For her, it was entertainment.

Later, when she and Greg were in bed, she asked him

what he thought about her best friend.

In the dark she heard his hesitation. Then after a moment he said, "He was nothing like I expected."

Julienne started to question him further, but something stopped her, probably a mixture of her loyalty to Daniel and her like for this man in bed beside her. She did not want the conflict, so she left it alone.

Instead, Julienne slid one leg in between his and found just the spot where her head fit on his chest.

She answered sleepily, "I am glad you two finally met."

Then they both went to sleep.

The Oklahoma song ended just as Daniel set a plate of food down in front of her and freshened up her coffee. Julienne began to dig into her scrambled eggs. Something about being at the beach always gave her a bigger appetite. Plus, she was still lost in her thoughts.

She glanced up to see Daniel's eyes focused on his own plate of food. Julienne scooped up some eggs onto the buttered toast and thought back to the first time she met Daniel's Tara. She was nothing like Julienne expected, either.

Julienne was home for a few days from OK State in the fall of 1997. She went there first because they had a great master's program in technical writing, but also because her dad had gone to school there. In a small way, it made her feel closer to her dad. It was a connection, at least. In Oklahoma they had fall break. In Texas they did not. Julienne was happy to have a break from her master's program even though she still had a paper to write.

Her aunt and uncle were happy to see her, and of course, she planned on catching up with Daniel.

It was a Thursday night. All the text said was

"Riverside," but Julienne knew it meant to come meet Daniel at the hole-in-the-wall bar.

Julienne ran a brush through her hair, put on a little lip gloss, and headed out. She had on jeans, flip-flops, and a white tank. With an olive complexion and plenty of time in the sun the past summer, Julienne looked tan and comfortable.

When she parked in the gravel lot, she texted Daniel "here." He met her at the door. Before she could say hello, he picked her up and twirled her around. He put her down and gave her a final squeeze before letting go. Julienne was laughing.

They had not seen each other since August when she had left for OK State. This was the longest they had ever gone without seeing each other since they had met. Sam Houston had been just an hour away and they saw each other all the time when she was working on her bachelor's degree, but now Julienne was eight hours away.

Daniel grabbed her hand and dragged her inside. The bar was full of dark wood and dim lights, and Kip Moore's "Beer Money" was playing on the jukebox, which made Julienne laugh since she had just enough cash to buy whatever longneck was on special tonight.

They went straight to the bar, where Julienne expected they would both order a drink, but instead Daniel tapped a blond on the shoulder.

The blond turned around and smiled. Her whole face smiled except for her eyes. Her light blue eyes, thick with mascara, remained cold.

Daniel made the introductions.

"Tara, this is my best friend, Julienne. And Julienne, this is my girlfriend, Tara."

Daniel was grinning from ear to ear while the women exchanged awkward handshakes.

There was a pause and then Julienne said, "How about a beer?"

Daniel signaled the bartender and the rest of the night ensued.

As the night went on, more people showed up and the local house band began to play. Julienne drank, danced, and watched Tara with a careful eye from across the long table where their group had settled.

Tara was a petite blond, which was just how Daniel liked them. Even in her heels, she didn't reach Julienne's 5'4" in her flip-flops. Tara's navy sheath dress was tasteful but boring. Her hair was teased and sprayed into a perfectly flipped-up bob.

Once, when she was staring, Daniel's brother David nudged her. She raised her eyebrows. He leaned in and whispered, "Don't stare for so long. Be more obvious."

She smiled. It was still weird for her to see David all grown up. He had always been the little brother that she and Daniel primarily left behind. He was a freshman in the engineering program at the University of Houston. He did not quite reach Daniel's height of 6'1", but while he was not quite as tall, he was much more filled out. He had dark blond hair like his brother's with eyes that stayed a constant shade of blue.

"Just taking it all in," she answered. "What do you think?"

"My initial reaction?" David threw out there.

Julienne nodded.

"She seems a little uptight."

Julienne nodded in agreement.

"But since she came along, my brother has actually been smiling, so," he shrugged, "who's to judge?"

Julienne nodded again. The band began to play and Julienne stood up.

"Come on, David," Julienne grabbed his hand. "Let's dance."

"Um, Jules," David said even as he got up and let her lead him to the dance floor. "I don't dance."

Julienne smiled and answered, "You do now."

As she dragged David onto the dance floor, she admonished him, "And don't call me Jules."

"But," he interjected. Julienne raised an eyebrow. "Okay, I guess Daniel owns that nickname and no one else."

Julienne smiled in affirmation.

She took the lead and Daniel laughed when they passed by. When the song ended, David followed her to the bar so she could buy them both a beer.

"Thanks, Julienne," David said when she handed him the bottle. He started to walk back to the table but stopped and turned around to add, "For the record, she's no you."

Julienne just laughed and David kept walking. She stayed at the bar to sip her beer and hopefully check out the new couple from afar.

Tara seemed to keep Daniel on a pretty short leash. Besides the initial greeting, Julienne hadn't gotten a chance to talk to Daniel the rest of the night. Daniel had been glued to Tara's side except for when he went to get himself another beer and Tara some fruity drink. Julienne wasn't having a bad time talking to everyone else. The beer was cold, and the music live, but her purpose in coming tonight was to catch up with Daniel.

Then, as luck would have it, the band began to play her favorite song: "Brown Eyed Girl."

Julienne immediately jumped up and went to Daniel's side of the table.

"Come on, Daniel," Julienne requested. "You owe me a dance."

Daniel stood but then looked over at his shoulder at Tara as if for permission. Tara shrugged her shoulders and looked away all at the same time. Julienne read indifference into those actions. She grabbed Daniel and led him to the dance floor just as the lead singer began singing, "Hey, where did we go?"

For a few minutes at least, Julienne had her Daniel back. They sang the words as Daniel twirled her, and they jumped up and down like pogo sticks during the sha-la-las. When the song ended, Julienne thanked Daniel and he walked straight back to Tara.

Julienne checked the time. It was a little after midnight. Julienne was tired and decided to bail. She left the Riverside without anyone noticing. Daniel had his eyes on Tara and David had his eyes on any girl who would pay attention to him.

Back at her aunt and uncle's, Julienne slept in her old room. When her head hit the pillow, her last thought before sleep was: I hate her.

The next morning Julienne was sleeping hard buried under the covers. What woke her was the bed actually moved. Her first thought while still half-asleep was earthquake. But Houston was hurricane country, so an earthquake did not exactly explain the shaking bed.

Julienne decided to open one eye and peek out from the covers to see what was causing the commotion. At the end of her bed bouncing up and down was her neighbor, Daniel.

He stopped bouncing to comment, "I forgot you woke up one eye at a time."

Julienne sighed and rolled over, putting her back to him. She was not a morning person, but of course, Daniel came over and of course, her aunt and uncle told him it was okay to barge in and wake her up. She felt his weight on the bed as he stretched out beside her on top of the covers.

"You left last night without saying a word," Daniel said.

Julienne continued to feign sleep.

"Jules," Daniel said in his best stern voice. "I'm not letting you go back to sleep."

Julienne with both eyes closed asked, "What time is it?"

Without pausing, Daniel answered, "Time for you to wake up."

Julienne could hear the smile in his voice because he knew she was acquiescing.

"You know this is my fall break," she protested. "I can sleep all day if I want."

Daniel shifted over to his side and closer to Julienne.

Then he whispered, "But your coffee would get cold."

Julienne opened one eye again.

"Coffee, what coffee?"

She could feel Daniel reach over her towards her nightstand. Then he held the cup up in front of her face.

"Your favorite, white chocolate mocha."

The smell was rich with a hint of sweetness and was very much inviting her to wake up.

Julienne rolled over onto her back and opened both eyes to look up at Daniel and the coffee.

"Well, you should've led with that," she declared as she began to sit up in bed.

Daniel laughed and handed her the coffee. He reached over and grabbed his coffee off the nightstand as well. Julienne eyed a plain white bag on the nightstand as well. She cocked her head towards the bag and raised her eyebrows in question.

Daniel kept a straight face and simply nodded his head.

"Seriously," she asked.

"Oh yea," Daniel answered.

Julienne reached for the bag with the familiar logo, knowing her favorite cinnamon rolls were in there. Three Brothers Bakery on Braeswood was one of their favorite places, but that meant Daniel had made a special trip to get her favorites. This made her wonder what Daniel was buttering her up for. He was going all out with her morning favorites. She took a sip of coffee and then a big bite of the cinnamon roll which was still warm and melted in her mouth. She moaned in pleasure.

Daniel just shook his head.

Julienne finished her bite and then asked, "What gives?"

Daniel sat back and rested his head against the quilted headboard. He took a sip of his coffee and then answered, "I wanna talk."

Julienne responded, "Okay, about what?"

"Tara," Daniel replied.

Julienne was glad she had just taken another bite of the cinnamon roll. She chewed slowly to stall, not sure what to say.

Daniel shook his head again and then without warning leaned over and gave her a forehead kiss.

When he sat back, he said, “God, I’m glad you’re home.”

Julienne smiled.

Daniel began. It turned out he wanted to talk and all Julienne had to do was listen. She leaned back and finished her coffee and roll. And she nodded occasionally while Daniel rambled on about his new girlfriend: Tara.

Daniel picking up their plates broke her reverie. The plates were mismatched, collected over the years from the different generations. Julienne’s plate was hunter-green, left over from a country-themed kitchen back in the ’80s. Daniel’s plate was pale pink with a turquoise trim, the remnants of a southwestern-themed kitchen. Every kitchen remodel was reflected in the plates here at the beach cabin.

Daniel asked, “What’s next?”

Julienne’s eyes widened as she realized she had no idea. She had not really planned past getting Daniel to the beach as a safe haven, but she had no idea what was next.

She shrugged.

Daniel grinned.

“Jules, the planner, has no plans,” he shook his head, chuckling as he said it.

Julienne shrugged again.

“Hit the beach,” Daniel half-stated, half-questioned.

Julienne nodded yes.

Daniel then said, “But I don’t have...”

Julienne interrupted by handing Daniel a bag that had a bathing suit, flip-flops, and sunscreen.

Daniel laughed.

"Never mind, Jules. Even when you don't plan, you plan," he said as he went off to change.

Julienne changed into the yellow bikini she had bought as well and then proceeded to coat herself with sunscreen. She put her hair in a low ponytail and pulled it through her baseball hat. She slipped on her flip-flops and then loaded their bag with supplies for the day. Daniel packed their cooler and off they went down to the beach.

The sun was out in full force but the slight breeze helped. It was a Monday so the weekend crowd had left and not many people were out. Daniel laid down on one of the towels and went back to sleep. His bruises looked better. He was still too skinny but maybe a whole week of eating at the beach would help. His skin was pale but the beach would help with that as well.

Julienne reached over and brushed his hair back out of his eyes. Daniel never stirred. Julienne then attempted to read her book about a rodeo cowboy and a college student, but her mind kept wandering.

That time at the Riverside, Julienne didn't really take Tara seriously, but two years later Tara was still around in a serious way.

Julienne was running late–not that being on time really mattered in Vegas. She was putting on a second coat of mascara when her phone vibrated. It was Daniel; he was down at the bar.

This time next week Daniel would be in his tuxedo for his wedding, but this weekend was his bachelor party and she, as his BFF, was the only girl here. Stepping back from the vanity to give herself a once over, she had to admit she looked like a girl tonight: gold sequin miniskirt, strappy heels, and a fresh pedicure with red toenails. She sprayed her perfume out in front of her and walked through the mist. Daniel always made fun of her for that, but it was a process that worked for her even if she did look silly. Then she grabbed her hotel key and clutch and went to go meet Daniel.

One overpriced dinner and one strip club later, the whole group was back at a bar in Caesar's, where they were staying. Daniel was sitting at the table sipping his whiskey. Julienne was coming off the dance floor ready to claim her $20 for convincing the security guard to dance with her.

She plopped down in her seat.

"Pay up," she said, holding out her hand.

Daniel just shook his head and gave her a twenty. Julienne's drink was empty so she grabbed Daniel's. Whiskey wasn't her first choice but it would do.

"Seriously," Daniel said. "My drink, too."

He just chuckled. His hair was slicked back. His brother, David, was right; since Tara, Daniel did smile more. He had put on weight in a good way. He was working steadily doing custom murals for people in their houses. He was making quite a name for himself. It turned out people would pay quite a bit to have their baby's nursery painted with a custom mural of their favorite nursery rhyme. Daniel claimed he was over rabbits and bears. He was keeping up with his own art on the side. Julienne was proud of him even if Tara continued to be frosty.

Julienne just smiled and sipped on what was left of Daniel's drink.

"Did I tell you how beautiful you look tonight?" Daniel asked.

Julienne looked away. Daniel's cousin was flirting with a girl at the bar and his brother had brought one of the strippers back with them and they were now grinding on each other on the dance floor.

Daniel reached over and with his hand turned her head back to face him.

"One day you will learn how to take a compliment," he declared.

Julienne just rolled her eyes and decided to change the subject.

"I see what your family members are up to, but where is everyone else?"

Daniel shrugged.

"We left two of them back at the strip club. My brother and cousin are both working on some girls and Tara's brother gave up and went back to his room."

"I think..." Julienne started but didn't finish. She was distracted by the song that had begun to play.

"What?" Daniel asked.

Julienne cocked her head towards the dance floor and said, "You hear that?"

Daniel listened and then broke into a smile.

"I think we need to dance," Julienne said as she grabbed his hand and led Daniel to the dance floor.

Prince's "Call My Name" was blasting through the speakers. While "Brown Eyed Girl" was her theme song in life, Prince was an artist that Julienne considered genius. "Call My Name" was maybe one of the best songs ever to slow dance to and she probably wouldn't have many more chances to dance with Daniel once he was married.

Daniel held her close. She always liked how he guided her with his hand on the small of her back. In her heels she reached his shoulder. She snuggled in and closed her eyes. They swayed to the music as Prince sang:

I heard your voice this morning
Calling out my name

Julienne still couldn't believe Daniel was getting married. It meant change and Julienne just wanted things to remain the same.

She held onto Daniel tighter as he sang softly into her ear:

And ever since that day I haven't wanted anyone but you

Julienne smiled at the words Daniel was singing. She was a little tipsy and tired. She all of the sudden found herself with the silly urge to cry and she wasn't sure why. Married or not, he would always be her Daniel.

"My Daniel," she thought.

"What did you say?" Daniel asked.

Julienne looked up at him. Her eyes looked extra big tonight thanks to the eyeliner and the second coat of mascara. She had not meant to say her thought out loud and smiled at her own ridiculousness. She put her hand on the left side of his face and continued to look into his eyes. Tonight, they were dark blue.

Julienne had always thought of him as hers. Regardless of boyfriends or girlfriends, they had always remained best friends. But now, he would be Tara's.

Julienne processed all of this while Daniel waited for an answer. She found she had none, so instead, she brushed a light kiss across his lips, leaving behind a red smudge on his lips as evidence of the interaction. Before she could see his reaction, she put her head back down on his shoulder.

He continued to hold her. They were not moving; instead, they were just holding each other in the middle of the dance floor. The last notes of "Call My Name" trailed off and a fast song took its place.

Julienne did not want to let go. She stayed a moment longer. Then she inhaled and took a step back.

"Keep dancing?" Daniel said as a question.

Julienne shook her head.

"Another drink?" Daniel asked.

Julienne nodded yes. Daniel moved away from her towards the bar. Julienne continued to stand there. She felt stupid for taking so long to realize Daniel was actually getting married. From the first night she met Tara, she never really took her seriously, but hello, she thought: We are in Vegas for his bachelor party and next week is his wedding.

Daniel would no longer be at her beck and call. There would be no more late-night runs to Dairy Queen for their favorite ice cream treat. There would be no more mornings where Daniel woke her up with coffee. There would be no more foot rubs which he made her beg for but in the end always obliged.

She could remember sneaking over to Daniel's to sweet-talk him into a foot rub plenty of Friday nights after having cheered at a football game.

Her neighbor would be a hard habit to break.

Julienne lasted until 2 a.m. and then she called it quits. She left Daniel waiting on his cousin, who was still working on the same girl at the bar. Daniel's brother had already left with an unnamed female.

When Julienne got to her room, she washed her face. Without makeup she looked like she was twelve. She put on a T-shirt and boxers. She plugged in her phone to charge and realized she had missed a call. It was from Greg.

This guy had been around long enough to be considered her boyfriend but was still new in her life. It took Julienne a while to get used to someone. His message said: I hope you are having a good time. Can't wait to see you tomorrow.

Greg was her ride home from the airport. Julienne smiled when she listened to his message, but then she frowned. She had not thought of Greg at all this trip. He simply had not been on her mind while she had been here. She was an inconsiderate girlfriend.

Julienne crawled into bed and turned off the lamp. She tried to turn her mind off and go to sleep, but it wouldn't come. Lying in the dark, she kept thinking about Daniel-dancing with Daniel, holding Daniel, kissing Daniel.

"My Daniel," she said for the second time that night out loud. She sat up in bed. Julienne wondered if she was losing her mind because she just had the craziest idea. She slipped on some flip-flops, grabbed her hotel key, and headed to Daniel's room, which was one floor below hers.

The elevator with its audacious gold accents seemed to be moving in slow motion, but the next thing she knew she was out and walking towards Daniel's room. Just as she raised her hand to knock, she heard the sounds.

A girl was shouting "Harder, harder."

This would've made Julienne laugh but this request was coming from inside Daniel's room. Julienne's face lost all color.

Then a male said, "Like this? You like this?"

Julienne's hand went to her mouth in astonishment. Julienne felt frozen to the spot even though she did not want to listen a second longer.

"What the hell am I doing?" she wondered to herself. She shook her head at herself and turned to go. She kept her eyes down and meant to walk quickly to the elevator. She was hoping for a quick getaway. Julienne only made it two steps before she ran into someone.

"I'm sorry," she murmured and stepped to the side to keep going, but a hand grabbing her wrist stopped her. Her first thought was to kick him in the nuts. That's what her uncle always told her, but then Julienne looked up, and holding her wrist was Daniel.

"Jules, what are you doing?" Daniel asked, still holding her wrist. His touch was warm and Julienne realized she was very cold standing there in the hallway in her shirt and boxers.

Julienne could not come up with an answer. She wished she was quicker on her feet. She wished she could come up with some clever answer which would essentially be a lie because she could not tell Daniel the truth. She could not tell him why she was really standing outside his hotel room.

At that moment, they both heard another moan come from the room. Daniel inclined his head toward the sound.

"Can you believe my cousin is in there nailing that girl from the bar?"

Julienne processed the information. Daniel's cousin was inside the hotel room with a girl. Daniel was outside in the hallway with her.

Daniel continued, "I just went up to your room. I can't

sleep in there. Were you looking for me?"

Julienne simply nodded her head yes.

"Great minds," Daniel chuckled as he guided her back to the elevator.

When they got back to her room, Daniel out of habit rearranged the pillows to accommodate their usual sleeping arrangement from when they were kids. Julienne just stood there.

"Jules, are you okay?" Daniel asked.

Julienne managed a smile as she slipped out of her flip-flops and into bed. Daniel got in the bed on the opposite side. Julienne switched off the lamp. Daniel squeezed her ankle. His hand was warm. Her feet were cold.

"You know what, Jules?" Daniel queried.

"What?" Julienne replied in a whisper in the dark.

"This could be our last sleepover. This time next week I will be married and waking up to Tara every day."

Julienne nodded her head in agreement and then realized Daniel could not see her.

"True," she said out loud.

Daniel continued with his reflection.

"Look at us, Jules, we are growing up."

Julienne could hear the smile in Daniel's voice.

"Speaking of significant others, how is your guy? Did he think it was weird, you being here this weekend?"

Julienne's face turned red at the mention of Greg. Even Daniel remembered to think of her boyfriend. She had not thought of him once. She certainly had not been thinking of Greg when she was outside of Daniel's room about to do God only knows what. Nope, Greg had not entered her mind at all. Greg was a good boyfriend and she, Julienne, was an awful girlfriend. Julienne was glad the lights were off and Daniel could not see her guilty face.

"Jules," Daniel shook her foot. "You still awake?"

"Yea," Jules muttered. "I'm here. Greg, he's good."

"Okay, sleepyhead," Daniel said. "I will be quiet. You go to sleep."

"Okay," Jules said even though she knew she wouldn't sleep.

"Jules," Daniel whispered.

"Yea."

"I'm glad you were here this weekend."

"Me, too," Julienne said and she meant it.

A few moments passed, then she felt his weight shift.

"Jules," he said again.

"Yea."

"I almost forgot," he said.

Julienne could tell Daniel was sitting up now.

"What?"

"Come here," Daniel requested.

Julienne sat up, not sure of what he wanted. Daniel's hand reached out and found her cheek. Then she felt him lean in and then, just as he had always done since they were kids, he gave her a kiss on the forehead.

Julienne sighed. This was normal. This was her friend Daniel taking care of her like he always had done.

"Good night," he said and laid back down.

"Good night," Julienne answered, but she never went to sleep.

Instead, she lay in the dark with her best friend on the opposite side and wondered how Daniel could be hers and yet not hers all at the same time.

And now here they were all these years later at the beach, and the sentiment still rang true: Daniel was hers but not hers.

CHAPTER 5

When Daniel woke up from his beach nap, he wanted to go out into the water. Daniel took off running and splashed his way up to his waist. Julienne took her time, entering the water inch by inch, letting her body get used to the cold of the gulf in contrast to the heat of the day.

"Come on, Jules," Daniel called to her.

Julienne shook her head and continued her snail's pace into the water. Daniel walked back towards her.

"Too slow," he said as he splashed her.

Julienne shrieked as the water hit her face, and in reaction splashed him back. A water war ensued, which ended with Daniel picking her up and carrying her out into the water.

Julienne used her loudest cheer voice, shouting, "Daniel, no," just as he dunked her under water. She came up swinging and instead he just held her in a bear hug. The water was up to her neck and she just gave in and held on to Daniel as the waves rocked them back and forth.

A few moments passed as they held on to each other. Daniel pulled them out deeper and she wrapped her legs around his waist and put her head on his shoulder. This reminded her of high school; Daniel was always throwing her into the deep end both literally and figuratively, but she could never be mad. He always kept her safe even if he was the one who put her in the unwanted situation to begin with.

Once in college they were at a bar in midtown listening to a band who did a mix of old and new rock. They were good enough to stay and listen to, especially with the beer specials that night. At one point they asked for a female to come on stage with them. The next thing she knew Daniel was picking her up and putting her on stage.

Julienne remembered being horrified. She couldn't sing and she had no business being on stage. She could feel how red her face was and when the lead singer asked for her name she was right back to a silent child. The long-haired singer nudged her; she choked out Jules. He handed her a tambourine and set her up with a microphone by the base player.

The whole time Julienne kept looking at Daniel, wondering what he had been thinking putting her up there. The lead singer asked if she was ready and she had no answer. Then they started playing.

With the first few notes, Julienne smiled. It was her favorite song. Then she knew. Daniel had set this up all along. He had insisted they come there that night. There was no way she just happened to be on stage and the band just happened to play her favorite song. She scanned the full bar. She knew none of these people but they were bouncing along to the beat.

At that moment Julienne took a breath and jumped right in. What she lacked in vocal talent, she made up for in enthusiasm. She played the tambourine and danced her way to each member of the band, singing with them on their microphones. Then she jumped off the stage and led the whole bar in a conga line to "Brown Eyed Girl."

When it was over, she punched Daniel in the arm, and then she jumped on him with a full-on hug.

"Whoa, Jules," Daniel said as he took a step back, not expecting the full force of her hug. Julienne wrapped her legs around him and whispered in his ear, "That was so much fun."

Daniel had just laughed and with Julienne in his arms ordered them another round. Julienne shook her head at that memory. That was Daniel both making her uncomfortable and beyond happy at the same time.

Daniel leaned over and whispered in her ear, "Did you buy this yellow bathing suit because you secretly still want to be Belle?"

Julienne's head snapped up as she came back to the present, and she narrowed her eyes at her neighbor.

"Sometimes, like right now," she said in a low voice. "I really don't like you."

This made Daniel throw his head back in laughter. Julienne let go of him and started making her way back to shore. Daniel continued to howl.

Julienne made it back to the towel and got herself some water from the cooler. Daniel was right behind her helping himself to a drink and lying back down on his towel.

"Jules, it's no big deal. I noticed you dressed me in green," he said as he batted his eyes.

"And still," Julienne said, turning her head away from Daniel. "I don't like you."

Daniel gave her ponytail a tug, but still she kept her

head turned and watched some imaginary fascinating thing to her right on the beach.

After a sip of her water, she begrudgingly admitted, “It was on sale.”

Daniel just laughed.

“Sure, Jules, you dressed us in your favorite colors because they both happened to be on sale.”

Julienne turned her head to face Daniel and narrowed her eyes.

“100% truth,” she stated.

Daniel just laughed more as he reached for a sandwich out of their bag of food.

He offered one to Julienne, which she took. They sat eating their sandwiches which she had made without even asking him what he wanted: ham and cheese with mustard. She was turkey and Swiss. They had eaten the same sandwiches since they were nine. Some things remained the same, like the comfortable rhythm of their friendship which they always seemed to be able to slip right back into no matter what. Some things, however, did not.

A blond walked by in a navy swimsuit with a tiny dog on a leash. The dog’s collar had rhinestones on it and the blond kept telling the dog to be quiet, but the rhinestoned pooch kept up its constant yapping.

A blond in navy reminded her of Tara which in turn brought back memories of Daniel’s wedding.

Julienne found herself in the middle of the dance floor at the country club. She was swaying to the music, but she really had no clue what song was playing. It had been a long day. Listening to the words, she heard Gary Allan sing:

Today I heard you got a new last name,
Sure didn't know it was gonna hit me this way,
And the radio just keeps on playing all these songs about rain

It wasn't raining but the song was right. Daniel's wedding had hit her hard, but here she was at the reception. She had made it through the event. Keeping busy had helped.

Julienne had the job of corralling Daniel and his friends away from golf and beer into some food and showers. Then she got them all to the church on time. While Julienne was not a bridesmaid, Tara had given her plenty of other duties to fulfill Daniel's request that his best friend be included in the wedding.

Julienne handed out the programs. Julienne escorted Daniel's dad and grandfather down the aisle to their seats during the processional. Julienne read a piece of scripture Tara had chosen during the ceremony.

The wedding met all the country club requirements. And Julienne hated to admit it, but the whole event was beautiful. Through it all Daniel beamed at Tara, and Tara beamed at whoever was taking her picture.

Tara wore a traditional ball gown complete with a tulle skirt and a sparkly bodice. Tara's bridesmaids wore pale pink. The color scheme throughout the country club was various shades of pink. When Julienne asked Tara what she needed to wear, thinking she needed to match the carefully planned color scheme, Tara just rolled her eyes.

This meant Julienne was instead wearing a full-length red halter gown cut low and slit high in all the right places. Diamond studs and a diamond bracelet capped off the look. The jewelry belonged to her mother and she was glad to have an occasion to wear the pieces. Julienne wore her hair in a messy updo to show off the low back of her dress and give a glimpse of her tattoo.

Daniel always liked a red dress and if she was being honest with herself, Julienne wanted to look good at Daniel's wedding.

Julienne lifted her head to see Daniel twirling Tara on the dance floor. He winked at her. Julienne put her head back down.

"Tired," his voice asked.

"Yes," she replied.

"Long day," he asked again.

"Very," she answered.

"I'm glad you asked me to be your date," he continued.

She was glad Greg was her date, too, because she would not want to be at this wedding solo.

"I like this red dress," Greg said as the hand on her back held her tighter.

Julienne looked up at his light brown eyes and smiled. Greg also had light brown hair, which was wavy. He had just gotten a haircut and she discovered that she liked his hair just a little longer. Greg had dressed up for the wedding tonight, breaking out a charcoal grey suit and a blue and grey tie. He looked nice and she was glad to be there with him on the dance floor.

"But you know what else," he queried.

Julienne shrugged her shoulders, still maintaining eye contact as they continued to sway.

"I love you," he said with a smile.

Julienne quit swaying even though the Gary Allan song continued to play. She paused to absorb what Greg had just said. Her best friend Daniel had just gotten married to a girl she did not like, but standing in front of her was the man she was dating declaring his love. Maybe, just maybe all was as it should be.

Julienne did not respond with words, but instead leaned in and gave Greg, the man who loved her, a kiss.

Julienne shivered at the memory. Daniel put his hand on her back. It felt warm and he took it away too soon.

"Cold?" he asked.

Julienne did not answer right away.

"Want to get back in the water?" he asked with a smirk.

Julienne shook her head no.

She grabbed some chips and absentmindedly began to munch on the Cheetos. Daniel helped himself to her bag as well. Daniel reminisced about eating Cheetos when they were kids, but Julienne's mind wandered back to weddings.

Daniel's wedding had been hard because at the time she did not know how that would change their friendship, but her wedding had been hard as well for different reasons.

A year after Daniel's wedding, Julienne found herself in the foyer of a church willing herself not to pass out. Her chest was tight and the sound of ocean waves was in her ears, meaning whenever someone spoke to her, they sounded muffled. She had lost feeling in her fingers and toes. This was probably not how the bride should be feeling on her wedding day.

"Canon in D" had just begun and the first bridesmaid was walking down the aisle. Julienne was wearing a strapless lace dress fitted through the hips and with a slight flare at the bottom. Her hair was parted on the side and pulled back in a low bun. The cathedral-length veil meant the train and was coming off as soon as the ceremony was over because she was sure someone would step on it at the reception. She wore her mother's pearl earrings and around her neck was the pearl necklace Daniel had given her the night before at the rehearsal dinner. He said Tara's father had given her pearls for her wedding, and Daniel thought Julienne should have pearls as well.

The gift was the perfect example as to why Julienne had named Daniel her best man in lieu of a maid of honor. Once again, her neighbor had given her the perfect gift without her even realizing she would need wedding pearls.

With one hand, Julienne held on to her bouquet of yellow roses, her favorites. Her other hand kept touching her pearls. Off to one side was her uncle, looking extremely out of place in a tuxedo since his typical clothing was plaid and denim. However, he was smiling. He kept telling Julienne how proud he was to walk her down the aisle.

On her other side was Daniel, also in a tux. He looked very handsome with his hair brushed back. Against the black of his tuxedo, his eyes looked dark blue.

Daniel put a warm hand on Julienne's bare shoulder. He leaned in and whispered, "Breathe."

Julienne just nodded.

Daniel came around to stand right in front of her. He took her hand from the pearls and held it.

"You look beautiful," Daniel said.

Julienne nodded.

"Don't be nervous," Daniel continued. "Forget all those

other people. Just look at Greg and remember I am right by your side."

Julienne nodded.

"Jules, you do love him, right?" Daniel asked for confirmation.

Julienne nodded.

"Then you can do this," Daniel declared. He gave her hand a squeeze and whispered, "Your eyes are the eyes of a woman in love."

Julienne just smirked at the *Guys and Dolls* reference and said, "Okay, Sky Masterson."

Daniel then went to stand behind the last bridesmaid.

Daniel had been so happy when Greg proposed. All he could do was talk about how happy he was being married and now Jules would experience the same. Julienne resisted change and marriage was a huge change. On the other hand, she would find no better man than Greg, and if Daniel could get married so could she.

Julienne's uncle took her hand and they went to stand behind Daniel. Once Daniel made it to the altar, the wedding march would begin and her uncle would take her down the aisle to be married.

Right as Daniel began to walk, he turned his head over his shoulder and said to Julienne, "Don't make me say I do for you."

He finished his comment with a wink and then took off. This made Julienne giggle. With the laughter, she felt herself begin to relax. Many times throughout her life Daniel had done her talking for her, but today was manageable. Today, she just had to say two words, "I do."

The rest of the evening was a blur that she could only piece together afterwards thanks to the pictures.

Julienne remembered Greg smiling from ear to ear as she walked down the aisle. She recalled her aunt shedding a few tears as her uncle handed her off to Greg.

The reception was dominated by lots of hugging and dancing. Julienne danced with Greg to a slow country song he had picked out. Then she danced with her uncle. Then they cut the cake, a three-tier monstrosity that Greg had picked out as well. Julienne didn't even like cake, but she wanted Greg to be happy. Then Daniel grabbed her for a dance. The DJ played Van Morrison's "Tupelo Honey" and Julienne remembered resting her head on Daniel's shoulder and just swaying. Then the song ended and her aunt grabbed her to say hello to some distant relatives. At the end of the night, Julienne was starving because she never had the chance to sit and eat.

When she and Greg were headed for the limo and bubbles filled the air, someone grabbed her from behind. As her feet left the ground, she looked down to see she was being twirled around by Daniel. When he put her down, he gave her a final squeeze.

"My Jules is married," Daniel declared.

His hair had fallen forward and his breath revealed the beers he had been drinking. His grin was still the same from the first day she had met him as a little boy. Everything about him was familiar to her.

Julienne stood on her toes to give him a kiss on his forehead and then said, "Don't worry. You will always be my neighbor."

Greg grabbed her hand and then they were in the limo on the way to the airport.

Later, Julienne realized Tara did not stick around. Julienne remembered Tara's frosty stare from the church pew. She also noted Tara was wearing red, which actually made Julienne smile. Red overpowered Tara's pale complexion and light hair, but Julienne appreciated the point she was making. In the pictures from the reception there was no Tara. Daniel sat at the family table with her aunt and uncle.

Tara's absence did not hurt Julienne's feelings at all, but she felt bad for Daniel that his wife had deserted him at the wedding of his best friend. In the end, all that mattered was Daniel's presence. Daniel had calmed her nerves and seen her through the whole event.

In the limo, she remembered holding Greg's hand and exhaling. Now she could breathe and hope she had done the right thing.

Sitting next to Daniel, finishing her chips, she took a breath. At the beach with Daniel like this, she could breathe. With Daniel, she could always breathe easy.

CHAPTER 6

When they were done eating, Daniel lay back down. He had one leg propped up and one arm over his eyes but he stayed awake. Julienne decided to ask.

"So," she said with trepidation, "What was it this time?"

Daniel started to protest the qualifier this time but stopped. Julienne knew as well as he did his reckless escapades were usually triggered by something he couldn't handle, so instead he did something destructive.

Daniel flipped over onto his stomach and with his head facing away from Julienne said in a low voice, "Tara is pregnant."

All Julienne could say in response was, "Oh."

She should not have been surprised because for Daniel most roads led back to Tara. Babies were a sensitive subject for Julienne. Picturing Tara pregnant for the first time reminded Julienne of the first time she had been pregnant.

A little over a year into her marriage to Greg, Julienne lay in the dark. The curtains were closed and she wasn't sure what time it actually was nor did she have the energy to care. She pulled the covers tighter around her shoulders and was drifting back to sleep when she heard voices.

"Thanks for coming," said one male voice.

"No problem," answered the other manly voice.

"I've got to go in today, but I didn't want to leave her alone."

"Happy to help."

"She won't talk," continued the first voice.

"Okay."

"I mean not at all."

"Okay."

"Well, her aunt and uncle said when she was a kid, well, they said to call you."

"Greg, I got this."

Then silence. Julienne waited. She wanted to be left alone. Julienne rolled over to her side and went back to sleep.

Later the sound of the bedroom door opening woke her. It could have been minutes or it could have been hours. She did not know. He crawled in bed with her and put his arms around her. She exhaled. At least with Daniel here, she could breathe. At least breathing wasn't such a burden.

After a few moments, Daniel said, "Jules, I love you with all my heart, but you kind of smell. I'm putting you in the shower."

Julienne's eyes opened wide. Her first reaction was to protest. Her second reaction was to laugh at the absurdness of her neighbor right now in this situation. In the end, all she did was nod her head.

Daniel scooped her up and carried her to the

bathroom. Julienne's bathroom was all black and white tile. Black and white pictures from her and Greg's trip to Paris added to the décor. Versailles, Notre Dame, and the Eiffel tower, all amazing moments from their trip, made her smile. Today, she was oblivious. Daniel set her down on the marble countertop and started the water. He checked to make sure the water was warm and then he threw Julienne in, clothes and all.

Startled Julienne opened her mouth and before she could speak was rewarded with hot water on her tongue. Daniel gave her a moment to acclimate and then he stuck his head in through the shower curtain.

"Your clothes were dirty too so I figured why not wash everything? I'm going to see about lunch. Can you handle getting clean?"

Julienne just stood there in her clothes with the water streaming off of her. She had no answer. She still could not believe he had just thrown her in like that.

Daniel continued, "Or do I need to get in there with you?"

This he asked with a smirk on his face. Today he had on a green shirt, probably in an effort to cheer her up because he knew she liked it when he wore green. When he smirked, his eyes looked like dark green emeralds.

Julienne shook her head no.

"Okay, wash your hair; wash everything. I'll be back to check on you."

Julienne just closed her eyes as the water continued to berate her. The shower curtain fell back into place. It was black and white toile, another nod to the Paris trip. Julienne heard the bathroom door open and shut. She wanted back in bed. She wanted to turn her mind off and standing under the water required her to do some thinking. She continued to stand as her wet clothes began to weigh her down.

After five minutes, Julienne relented and shrugged out of her clothes. Then she reached for the shampoo. Even after she was clean, she continued to just stand under the water until it ran cool.

When Julienne stepped out of the shower, she found Daniel had left her some clean clothes to put on, including an old Bellaire High T-shirt and some grey sweats.

Julienne came out of the bathroom to find Daniel stripping the sheets off the bed.

Daniel looked up, saying, "Those needed to be washed, too."

Julienne continued to stand there as he busied himself with the sheets. She had really wanted to crawl back in bed but that no longer looked like an option. Daniel walked off with the sheets and Julienne stared at the bare mattress.

When Daniel returned from starting the wash, Julienne was still standing there, unsure of what to do next.

Daniel went into her bathroom and came out with a brush. He gathered her tangled hair and started at the bottom, working his way up until all the tangles were gone. Julienne remembered when she was little her hair was all the way down her back. Her dad used to brush her hair every night before bedtime. Julienne had not thought of that memory in a long time. She kept the memories of her parents locked up tight.

In that moment Julienne missed her parents, especially her dad. She wished he was with her in that moment to make everything better for his little girl like only a dad can do.

It was this thought that made her cry. Just one tear leaked out but that was enough to start the stream. She had not cried at all during this whole ordeal. She had tried so hard not to cry. Crying meant feeling, and Julienne did not want to feel the loss. She did not think she could bear it.

She had survived losing her parents, she had survived losing her dog, but she did not think she could survive this: Miscarriage.

Julienne had lost their baby.

Greg was at work, but she was stuck in neutral. At least until she thought of her dad.

Those first few silent tears leaked out. Julienned wiped them away. Daniel quit brushing her hair and turned her around. She could not make eye contact, but she could not stop the tears either.

Daniel just held her and let her cry. The first few silent tears led to huge sobs which escaped her. Her whole body felt like it was shaking but Daniel with his strong arms held on until she was done crying. He held her tight and whispered the words to one of her favorite songs:

I took my love, I took it down
Climbed a mountain and I turned around
And I saw my reflection in the snow-covered hills
'Til the landslide brought it down
Oh, mirror in the sky
What is love?
Can the child within my heart rise above?
Can I sail through the changin' ocean tides?
Can I handle the seasons of my life?

At that point, they were on the ebony wood floor. Daniel was rocking Julienne back and forth as she continued to hiccup and eke out the last of her tears. The sound of the doorbell made Julienne jump.

Daniel just patted her on the back, saying, "That would be lunch."

Then Daniel gave her a forehead kiss and headed to the front of the house. Julienne returned to the bathroom to splash water on her face.

The image in the mirror was not good. Her face was red from crying. Her eyes were swollen and the dark circles under her eyes looked cavernous. Julienne took a breath. She pulled her damp hair into a messy bun on top of her head.

Her stomach growled as her nose registered the smell of pizza. For the first time in three days, Julienne felt like eating.

She did not feel like talking, but she thought she could manage food so she went to seek out Daniel and the pizza.

Julienne shivered again at this particular memory even though nothing but sunshine was out on the beach. Daniel still lay there with his head averted. Julienne decided to keep asking questions.

"How far along?"

"Ten weeks."

"How did you find out?"

"Her mother called me."

"Really?" Julienne asked, her voice rising on the second syllable.

"Yea," Daniel affirmed, turning his head towards hers. "I was surprised, too. She said she thought I deserved to know and didn't want me to hear it in a roundabout way."

"Well," Julienne paused. "That's different."

That was all Julienne could think to say. Tara was a master at the roundabout game, which was part of the reason Daniel was so tortured.

About a year after the miscarriage, Julienne was leaving the doctor's office with a smile on her lips. The sun was shining as if to match her mood. Julienne had a thousand thoughts in her head all at the same time and they were interrupted by her phone ringing.

Before she could even say hello, Daniel was already talking.

"It's all gone," Daniel said, his voice just above a whisper.

"What?" Julienne responded, holding the phone in one hand and her car keys in another. She had good news to share, but first she had to figure out what was wrong with Daniel.

"Jules," Daniel repeated himself. "It's all gone."

Julienne pushed the unlock button and was navigating getting into her emerald green car while talking to Daniel. She was dying to tell him her news, but to be fair, she should tell Greg first. She tried to focus on what Daniel was saying.

She turned the key in the ignition and asked, "What's all gone, Daniel?"

"Everything," he paused. "I came home early to surprise her, and it's all gone."

"Tara," Julienne stated as she began to process Daniel's news.

"Tara," Daniel declared.

"I'm on my way," Julienne said, with all her previous thoughts about what to do with her news gone and her only focus on her neighbor, Daniel.

Twenty minutes later Julienne pulled up to his house. She found Daniel standing in the middle of his living room. His hair was everywhere, a sign he had been running his fingers through it. He was clutching a bouquet of pink roses. He turned his head to look at Julienne but said nothing. His button-down shirt had come untucked from his slacks. It wasn't often Julienne saw him dressed in business attire since he was generally in jeans with paint stains.

Julienne checked all the rooms; Daniel had not been exaggerating. All her stuff, all their furniture minus a mattress was gone.

"Daniel, what happened?" Jules asked.

Daniel raked his hands through his dark blond hair and shook his head.

"This morning when I was walking out the door to work, she said, I'm not happy. I gave her a kiss on the cheek and said I hate to hear that. Let's talk tonight."

Daniel started pacing as he was describing what happened.

"So, all day I thought: poor Tara. I've been working so much. I'm going to get her flowers. I'm going to spend some real time with her tonight and rub her feet, bubble bath, whatever she wanted."

Daniel turned to look at Julienne.

"So, then I came home to this."

He held his arms out wide, indicating the empty house. The flowers fell from his left hand and scattered on the wooden floor. The roses were pink, Tara's favorite color. The delicate pink petals fell away from the bud and just laid there on the floor. The flowers were broken just like

Daniel's marriage.

Julienne did not say anything. She had no idea what to say so she remained silent.

Daniel continued pacing.

"She didn't say I want a divorce or I'm moving out," his voice was getting louder. "She said I'm not happy."

He kicked at the flowers for emphasis.

"Jules," Daniel said, making eye contact with his best friend. "In what universe does I'm not happy mean this?"

"I," Julienne stumbled, "I don't know."

"Fuck, Jules," he said in desperation. "It's all fucking gone."

He scooped up some roses and threw them. They didn't go very far, which only served to anger him more. He looked around, presumably for something else to throw, but there was nothing else available. The house was empty and the emptiness said it all.

Julienne touched his arm. Daniel grabbed her hand. They stood there in silence. Daniel continued to process the emptiness.

Julienne asked the obvious, "She's not answering her phone?"

Daniel shook his head no.

"I'm going to make a few phone calls," Julienne declared. Daniel continued to hold her hand. "I will be right back," Julienne squeezed his hand. Daniel let go in assent.

Julienne let herself out the back door onto the patio. Even the patio table and chairs were gone. However, Tara had left behind the bench Daniel had made for them when they moved into this house.

"What a cold-hearted bitch," Julienne thought. Then

she pulled out her phone and sat down on the bench Daniel had built for his wife.

First, she called Greg to let him know she would be getting home late that night.

Second, she called Tara. The call went straight to voicemail. Julienne had a lot she wanted to say but she kept her message simple: Tara, this is Julienne. Call me.

Third, Julienne called Julienne's parents. Julienne had met them several times. Her overall impression was they were nice people even if they had raised a spoiled daughter. She called them because she knew Tara did not make a move without her mother. Julienne figured talking to them was the next best thing to speaking with Tara.

The sun had set and a slight breeze was blowing. Daniel and Tara had a huge backyard with a mix of oak and pine trees. There were markers in the middle of the yard outlining the pool Tara wanted to have put in before the summer. Julienne shook her head, figuring no pool now. Daniel had just gone along with the idea to make Tara happy.

Speaking of happy, Julienne had news that would make everyone smile, but like the setting sun, her rays of happiness would have to wait for the moment. Instead, Julienne called Tara's parents. The phone call lasted four rings then went to the answering machine; this time Julienne left a longer message:

"Hi, this is Julienne, Daniel's friend. Please tell Tara to call him. Please tell her if she is leaving him, he at least deserves a conversation. Tell her it's pretty chicken shit to just take everything without a word. Tell her," Julienne took a breath, "just tell her to call him, and I apologize for cursing."

Ending the call, Julienne shook her head at herself. This wasn't her fight, but he was her neighbor.

Before walking back inside she made one more phone call to Daniel's dad. She got his voicemail as well; no one seemed to be answering their phone tonight. She told Daniel's dad to be sure to check on his son because he would need his dad.

Julienne walked back inside and Daniel was sitting on the floor, head in his hands. He had kicked off his shoes and his legs were crossed in front of him. For a moment she saw the young boy he once was and her heart ached for him because she knew as a little boy, he never got over his mother leaving him; now he would never get over his wife leaving, either.

"Daniel," Julienne said in a calm voice. Daniel did not respond. Julienne stepped out of her sandals and sat down beside him. She put her hand on his shoulder. He reached for her hand and pulled her into his lap. He held her tight and she returned the embrace. They began to rock.

"She's gone," Daniel said in a hoarse whisper.

"I know," Julienne responded, rubbing his back.

"She's gone," Daniel said again, as if for confirmation. Then he began to cry.

The next day Daniel was served with papers. It was obvious Tara had not been happy for a while and Daniel was not happy about being blindsided.

Daniel's response to being served divorce papers was getting drunk. By the time Julienne arrived at the Riverside, Daniel was beyond drunk. She tipped the bartender for giving her a call and headed over to Daniel, who was stumbling his way through a two-step by himself on the dance floor while Waylon came through the jukebox singing about a good-hearted woman. Julienne shook her head at the irony.

"Jules," Daniel gestured with his hand. "Come dance with me."

"Is that what you are doing," Julienne smirked in response. "It's hard to tell."

"You're funny," Daniel said, continuing his pseudo dance. "It's a good quality. I like that about you."

Julienne grabbed his hands. The smell of his favorite whiskey, Jameson, was strong. It seemed to emanate from every pore in his body. Julienne had to turn her head to take a breath. Then she faced Daniel with a forced smile.

"I have a lot of good qualities, Daniel. Come on."

Daniel at 6'1" always had to look down at Julienne's 5'4". This time his eyes went past her face to her chest.

"Yes, you do, Jules. You have lots of good qualities."

Julienne rolled her eyes and lifted his chin.

"Seriously, Daniel, let's go."

Daniel put his arm around her shoulders, saying, "Okay, okay."

Julienne was glad he acquiesced. She had expected more of a struggle.

As they walked out of their favorite hole-in-the-wall bar, Daniel, in the loudest drunk whisper ever, asked, "Jules, are your boobs getting bigger?"

Julienne just kept walking while the couple at the nearest table laughed.

Julienne stopped at the nearest Jack in the Box on the way home and got Daniel some tacos. She hoped the grease would help soak up the alcohol. When they got to his house, she made him take some aspirin. Then she put him to bed on the mattress Tara had left behind.

Daniel's mind was all over the place and so were his remarks.

"Jules, Jules, she's gone," he would mumble.

In the next breath he would say, "Jules, Jules. I really think your boobs are bigger. I bet Greg likes that."

Then he would say, "Jules, divorce papers. I got served today."

All the while Julienne got his shoes off and found a blanket to go with his mattress.

Daniel seemed to mumble himself to sleep. When his eyes were closed and his breathing even, she took that as her cue to leave. Julienne stood up and started to tiptoe out of his room.

"Jules," Daniel called out.

"Yes, Daniel," she answered.

"Will you stay?"

Julienne did not respond right away. They were not nine years old anymore. Greg, her husband, was waiting.

"Please," Daniel added.

"Of course," Julienne said. She slipped her shoes off. Daniel moved over. She laid down like they had back when they were kids with their heads on opposite sides.

"Jules," he said again.

"Yes, Daniel."

Through the moonlight streaming in through the windows with no curtains thanks to Tara, Julienne could see Daniel take his finger and point to his forehead. She couldn't help but smile and then she obliged with a forehead kiss.

"Better?" she asked.

"Better," he responded.

Julienne lay back down. Daniel went to sleep holding

her right foot. Julienne lay there for an hour, her thoughts all over the place. Lying there reminded her of their childhood and all the times Daniel helped her go to sleep. Looking around at the bare room only made her contempt for Tara grow. Her boobs, which were bigger and sore, only reminded her of the secret she was still holding onto. Her mind continued to ping-pong back and forth. The sounds of Daniel snoring meant he was really asleep this time and she left unnoticed.

When she got in her car, the radio was playing Eric Church:

It's over when it's over
Ain't it baby, ain't it
Rips ya like a dagger,
Can it baby, can it
Wish we could do it over
Damn it baby, damn it

Julienne could not agree more as she drove home to her husband while her best friend slept alone.

Julienne would never forgive Tara for the way she left Daniel. All these years later, he was still affected by her.

"Do you want to talk about it?" Julienne asked while she switched from sitting to lying down on her towel.

She turned her head to face Daniel.

"Not really," he answered.

"So, your reaction to this news was to get super drunk and thrown in jail?"

Daniel shut his eyes and then let out a sigh.

When he made eye contact again, he admitted, "Yep, pretty much."

Julienne continued, "And you know this fits your usual pattern?"

Daniel started to turn his head away from her, but she reached out and put her hand on his back. His skin was warm. She needed him to face this, not turn away.

Another sigh and he put his head back where it had been resting on his forearms facing her.

"Yes, Jules, I know."

Julienne pushed his hair back out of his eyes.

"I just hate to see her continue to have so much power over you."

"She doesn't."

Julienne arched an eyebrow.

"Okay, she did," Daniel conceded. "But she doesn't anymore. It was just the baby. She and I were supposed to have babies. I want to be a dad."

"And you will one day. You will be a great dad," Julienne encouraged.

Daniel laughed.

"What?" Julienne asked.

"You forgot the if, Jules. You mean you will be a good dad if you ever get your shit together."

With that, Daniel did turn his head away from her. Julienne remained silent. The guy who got thrown in jail was probably not dad material, but the other Daniel, her Daniel, would be an amazing father.

CHAPTER 7

Julienne put on some more sunscreen and adjusted their umbrella to provide more coverage while Daniel continued to lie there. The sun continued to move across the sky as they were spending all day out there.

The Daniel in front of her now reminded her of the Daniel he had been immediately following the divorce.

After Tara's dramatic exit, Julienne had to wait till that Friday to take Greg out for dinner at his favorite steak place. The arrival of a baby bottle with his beer signaled the good news.

Greg had simply grabbed the beer at first and took a sip. Then he zeroed in on the baby bottle the waitress had placed down as well.

His eyes grew big. He picked up the bottle, which was yellow with a white bow around the neck. He stared at it like he did not know what it was. Then he put it back down.

"Julienne?" he had said her name in a question.

She had just smiled and nodded her head.

"Really?" he said, still questioning.

"Yes," Julienne said, still smiling.

Greg jumped out of his chair and put both hands in the air. People seated near them were giving him strange looks, but Greg exclaimed, "I'm going to be a dad."

The patrons clapped while Greg grabbed Julienne from her chair and hugged her.

The reveal had gone better than expected and she knew Greg deserved this moment. The rest of the night people kept coming up and shaking his hand. The restaurant gave them dessert on the house and Greg never stopped smiling.

Julienne knew the miscarriage had been hard on Greg as well and she had retreated into herself as a way of coping. She was glad to be able to make him smile. They both agreed to keep the baby news to themselves until she was further along. Right now, she was only eight weeks.

The last time she had miscarried at 14 weeks. Julienne made a deal with Greg that at week 16, he could take out an ad in the *Houston Chronicle,* but until then it would be their little secret.

Later that night in bed, Greg commented, "I thought your boobs were getting bigger."

Julienne laughed, saying, "Daniel said the same thing."

Greg moved a little away from her, asking, "Does he know?"

"About the baby?" Julienne asked, her voice rising a little. "Of course not. You are my husband. You get the news first, silly goose."

Julienne nudged him to emphasize the silly goose. Greg moved back closer and kissed her shoulder.

"I know," he said, "but girls tell their best friends stuff, and he is your best friend."

"Okay," Julienne responded, resting her head on Greg's chest, "but no one knows but us."

"Are you going to tell him?"

"I don't know," Julienne sighed. "He is in such a bad place right now."

"You don't think he can handle your good news?" Greg asked.

Julienne didn't answer.

Greg asked another question, "So how was he today?"

"Well, he didn't sound too drunk on the phone. His dad was over there. He did ask to go to some estate sales tomorrow."

"Really," Greg commented. "You know furniture is community property. She should return some of it."

Julienne appreciated Greg's comment. It was a show of support for Daniel.

"He says he doesn't want it. He says he is going for vintage eclectic."

"No, he didn't."

"Okay, he didn't. I did. It's better than buy some crap at a yard sale. Buying some furniture is a small step toward acceptance."

"True," Greg said. "Okay, enough about that. We're in bed, you're pregnant, and I love you."

Julienne smiled into the dark and hugged Greg.

"I love you, too."

Greg brushed her lips with a kiss and off to sleep he went. Sleep did not come right away for Julienne. She was glad to have had a night of just the two of them reveling in their good news, but the image of her neighbor drunk on his mattress stayed with her.

The next morning Kenny Chesney's "Come Over"

accompanied her to Daniel's house:

I told you I wouldn't call, I told you I wouldn't care
But baby climbing the walls gets me nowhere
I don't think that I can take this bed getting any colder
Come over, come over, come over, come over, come over

It felt like she had been coming over to Daniel's house a lot lately. This morning she arrived with coffee in hand for Daniel, hot chocolate for her. Daniel's black truck was in the driveway, but he didn't answer her knock.

She figured he was still sleeping. To be clear, she figured he was probably sleeping off his hangover. So far, drinking had been his only response to being served divorce papers.

Julienne waited a moment longer and then got out her key to Daniel's house. This was one of the perks of being a best friend; she had a key. The house was a typical ranch-style from the 1950s but Daniel had updated it with new shutters and the addition of a proper front porch. They had painted the brick a stark white and Tara had chosen navy for the shutters. The overall look was clean and crisp.

Julienne let herself in and headed straight to his bedroom. Halfway down the hall, she heard moaning.

At first, Julienne thought maybe Daniel was crying but the moans were low and guttural; no keening there.

She continued toward his bedroom but at a slower pace. The door was ajar about three inches, just enough to sneak a peek. Julienne peered inside and almost dropped the coffee at what she saw.

Daniel was on his knees at the foot of the mattress. A light sheen of sweat was on his back and his hawk tattoo appeared to be soaring with the movement.

Daniels' bare butt was undulating back and forth. Every time he would thrust into the faceless girl he would grunt. It reminded Julienne of a tennis match.

The girl's legs, long and pale, were spread eagle in the air. Every time Daniel thrust into her, she curled her toes and gave a little moan. Julienne did not mean to stand there and stare, but the scene was both jarring and mesmerizing at the same time. She felt like she was twelve all over again watching porn for the first time with Daniel; it had been some video with bad music and a pizza delivery man. They had snuck the video from his dad. Julienne couldn't look away then either.

Julienne heard the girl say something but it was unintelligible. She wondered what the girl was saying.

At the same time Julienne was wondering, Daniel prompted the spread-eagle girl, "Louder."

On the next thrust the faceless girl said, "What a big dick."

Daniel prompted her again with steel in his voice, "Louder."

This time the faceless girl gave it some volume and shouted, "Oh, what a big dick!"

This made Julienne giggle. At the sound of her laugh, Daniel turned his head.

Continuing to thrust, Daniel said, "Hey, Jules."

Julienne grinned and held up the coffee and her car keys. Daniel nodded his head. Julienne went back out to her Cadillac to wait. Greg had wanted her to buy a Camry or an Altima, but Julienne had met Daniel for lunch one day and two swirl margaritas later had come home with an emerald green Cadillac.

Julienne loved the car; Greg liked that he hadn't been bothered with the process even if she did not purchase what he had preferred. He had simply shrugged his shoulders and said, "It's your car, Julienne."

Meanwhile Daniel had stated, "If you are going to have a grown-up car, then it has to be something cool and classic like a caddy. It fits you, Jules."

Julienne had agreed. The car made her happy.

Ten minutes later Daniel strode out in blue jeans with wet hair slicked back. He got in the passenger side and she handed him his coffee.

With raised eyebrows, Daniel asked, "You enjoy the show?"

Julienne shook her head.

"Oh, what a big dick–really?" she giggled again.

Daniel grinned in return and with a wink said, "Well, darlin', it gets the job done."

Julienne started the car and asked, "Are you just going to leave her there?"

"Her ride is on the way," Daniel said, leaning back in the seat and taking a sip of the coffee.

"Will she even be able to walk," Julienne asked, backing out of the driveway, half-joking, half-serious.

"I'm thinking she might be a little sore," Daniel said, staring straight ahead.

Julienne shook her head and kept driving. Daniel picked up the list of estate sales Julienne had compiled.

"Thanks for doing this, Jules."

They drove in silence. Both sipped on their drinks. The first stop was about twenty minutes away.

After about ten minutes, Daniel turned down the volume on the radio and broke the silence, saying, "But really, Jules, did you like what you saw?"

Keeping her eyes on the road, Julienne took her right hand off the wheel and gave Daniel the finger.

Daniel burst out laughing and patted Julienne on the head.

At their first stop, Daniel bought an old leather sofa in great condition. It was only then they realized they should have brought Daniel's truck. They paid for the sofa and returned later with the truck. Daniel also purchased a bed frame with a headboard and a nightstand and a few more odds and ends. They ended the day at their favorite Mexican restaurant, where Julienne wolfed down chips and queso but declined a beer, opting for Sprite instead.

Daniel had bought some furniture, he was smiling, and he had checked rebound sex off the list. She almost told him her news but held back. He was having a good day and she wanted it to remain just his good day.

Looking at Daniel's back, his tattoo had faded slightly over the years but it was still an impressive piece of art. Julienne peered over him to see his eyes were closed. He was sleeping so much but she figured he needed it. She went to dip her toes in the water without fear of being dragged into the deep this time.

She walked out just a little bit and then sat in the water so the waves could lap over her. The salt water gently pushed and pulled as she just focused on breathing. She continued to remember Daniel's divorce.

One month after their estate sale shopping, Julienne was once again letting herself into Daniel's house. His truck was there, but he was not answering his phone. She had not heard from him in three days.

Greg had told her to be patient, not to overreact. Greg

kept reminding her Daniel was a grown man. Daniel could be anywhere.

But Greg did not know Daniel the way she did. His mother left when he was three. Now his wife had left him. Daniel was reacting by drinking and one-night stands.

Julienne was now twelve weeks pregnant. She was tired and every morning she was nauseous, but she welcomed it. Even though they were waiting to tell everyone, she was ready to tell Daniel; however, she had to find him first.

It was six p.m. on a Wednesday. All the lights were off in his house and the air smelled stale. Julienne turned on a lamp to survey the living room. The leather sofa they had found at the estate sale fit right into his house. She and Daniel shared a love of older homes with hardwood floors, high ceilings, and crown molding. The leather sofa fit the bones of the house much better than the streamlined modern sectional Tara had taken in the divorce.

Julienne wandered into the kitchen. The trashcan was overflowing with beer cans. On the counter sat a bottle of Jameson whiskey with about an inch of the amber fluid left in it.

Julienne kept waiting to hear sounds from the bedroom, thinking maybe she'd walked into a repeat from estate sale shopping. As she pushed the bedroom door open, the room was silent. Daniel's bed looked like it had been slept in, but no one was currently occupying it. Julienne checked the rest of the rooms–empty, dusty, no Daniel.

Julienne called Daniel again but it went straight to voicemail. She decided to strip the bed and wash the sheets. If she had to guess, they hadn't been cleaned since she first put them on the mattress for him.

Julienne walked out to the garage which had a nook for the washing machine and dryer. Daniel was lying face down on the concrete in a pool of dried vomit. Julienne froze and felt a tightening in her chest. Her mouth opened but no sound came out. Then she dropped the sheets and ran the short distance to Daniel.

Julienne kept repeating his name over and over: Daniel.

She tried to roll him over but it was hard because he was such dead weight. Daniel was pale and cold but he was breathing. Julienne kept saying his name as tears streamed down her face. Julienne fished her phone out of her pocket and called Greg but she was having a hard time explaining what was wrong through her tears.

"Julienne, Julienne," Greg said firmly. "I need you to slow down and tell me what's the matter."

Julienne paused. She wiped her face with the back of her hand and took a breath.

"It's Daniel. I need you to come over to his house now."

"Okay, Julienne, Okay. I'm on my way."

In Julienne's mind while she sat there with Daniel, "Into the Ocean" kept replaying over and over in her mind:

I'm just a normal boy
That sank when I fell overboard
My ship would leave the country
But I'd rather swim ashore
Without a life that's sadly stuck again
Wish I was much more masculine
Maybe then I could learn to swim

When Greg got there, Julienne was sitting cross-legged with Daniel's head in her lap. She had wiped him off as best she could with the bedsheets. She was still crying.

Greg just shook his head at the sight. With a little bit of a struggle, Greg got Daniel up and dragged him inside.

Julienne put the sheets in the wash and threw some fertilizer on the vomit.

Julienne found Greg standing in Daniel's bathroom. The shower was running.

"Is he-how is he?" Julienne stumbled through her inquiry.

"He's coming around," Greg said. "The cold water helped."

Julienne started to speak but Greg guided her out into Daniel's bedroom, leaving the bathroom door opened.

"Greg," Julienne sobbed stepping closer for a hug. "I thought he was dead."

She thought Greg would take her in his arms and offer comfort, but instead he stepped back. Then he started pacing. Julienne stood there eyes big; tears still falling. The only sound was the water from the shower.

Greg stopped pacing and when he faced her, he folded his arms across his chest and said, "Julienne, I am done"

Julienne just continued to stare.

"You are done," he declared, getting louder.

Julienne continued to stare, continued to let the tears fall down her face.

"I thought something was wrong with you," Greg continued. "I thought," and then he shook his head, not finishing the thought.

Greg looked down and then back at Julienne. Now he was shouting. "I won't have you dealing with this anymore. It's too stressful."

"Daniel's just going through a rough time," Julienne countered.

"Exactly," Greg confirmed, still shouting. "Daniel is going through a rough time, not you."

"What are you saying?" Julienne asked. She had quit crying and her arms were now folded over her chest.

"You have to stop this," Greg said.

This was the most he had ever raised his voice. She had never seen him this angry. They had disagreed before but never anything that a little space and a second conversation could not resolve. One of the things Julienne appreciated about Greg was how even-keeled he always was. Daniel called it predictable; either way, Greg was stable and Julienne needed that in her life.

"Stop what?" Julienne asked, feigning ignorance and appalled at his anger and lack of compassion for her and for Daniel.

"Rescuing him," Greg stated. "That is a mess in there," said Greg, pointing to the shower. "But," his voice continued to get louder. "It is not your mess."

With her arms still folded, Julienne stuck out her chin and declared, "He is my best friend." Then she added, quieter, "Who do you think rescued me?"

"This is no good for you," Greg continued.

Julienne continued to stand there.

Greg came right up to her and stated, "It's no good for you and it's no good for the baby."

Julienne started to speak, but she was interrupted by another voice.

"Baby," was heard off to the side.

Julienne and Greg both turned their heads. Neither

had noticed that the water had stopped. Standing in the doorway of the bathroom was Daniel, dripping wet with a towel wrapped around his waist. Julienne's eyes went straight to Daniel's ribs. They were poking out, almost demanding to be fed. He was too thin. His eyes were sunk in his face. He looked awful, but at least he was standing.

Daniel took a step toward her.

"Jules," he paused. "You're pregnant?" Daniel asked in a quiet voice.

Julienne nodded her head.

Daniel grabbed her and held her tight.

"A baby," he said again, still holding her. "I'm sorry," he whispered in her ear. "I'll do better."

All Julienne could do was nod her head and accept Daniel's wet embrace.

Daniel stood back, smiling.

"Greg, that's amazing," he said, reaching out his hand.

Greg's breathing was still slowing down from being angry, but he returned the smile and the handshake.

Daniel turned back to Julienne.

"How far along are you? How are you feeling? I knew your boobs were getting bigger."

An onslaught of questions and comments poured from Daniel's mouth.

Julienne stood there stunned. If she had known this would be Daniel's reaction to the news of the baby, she would have told him sooner. When she had first arrived that day, she thought he was dead; now with the shower and the news of the baby, he was reborn. Julienne had no response, but Greg intervened.

"First, how about you get dressed?" Greg suggested with a grin.

Daniel looked down and realized he was half-naked in a towel.

"Right, right. I'll get dressed," Daniel began to rummage through a pile of clothes.

Greg guided Julienne out towards the living room and called over his shoulder, "While you get dressed, how about I order some takeout?"

"Perfect," Daniel said as he turned to some clothes hanging in his closet.

"What do you want?" Greg asked.

"Let the pregnant lady decide," Daniel said, closing his door to finish getting dressed.

Julienne chose Chinese food. Shrimp fried rice and egg rolls were calling her name. Thirty minutes later all three of them sat down to a picnic in Daniel's living room. They ate, they laughed, and they only spoke of the baby.

In the end, she filed that night away in her good memory file of Daniel. Of course, this memory also lived in her bad memory file as well. Daniel had always been a constant paradox in her life. The juxtaposition of hard and easy, good and bad, laughter and tears.

Julienne smiled at that memory. The sand shifted next to her and she looked up to see Daniel beside her. She continued to smile. He put his hand on her shoulder and joined her, sitting in the water.

"I keep sleeping," he stated.

"You need it," Julienne said.

Daniel tugged on her ponytail, which was damp and full of salt and sand.

"What do you need?" Daniel asked.

Julienne cocked her head. She was ready to talk about Daniel some more, but not herself.

"Come on, Jules," Daniel continued. "We don't need to talk about me. We know my pattern. What about you? You came to the beach for me and I appreciate it, I do, but did you maybe need the beach as well?"

Julienne's immediate answer was no. The waves continued to lap at their feet. The beach was for Daniel. She hesitated, though. Reflecting on Daniel's life meant reflecting on hers as well. Their lives were just that intertwined.

She put her hands behind her and leaned back to feel the sun on her face and to talk to Daniel's back instead of his face.

"Well, why don't you tell me why I need the beach," Julienne said in a low voice.

"That's easy," Daniel answered. "You needed an escape."

"I do?"

"Oh yea, Jules, you do."

"Continue," Julienne prompted.

"From the outside looking in, you are leading the perfect middle-class life: Nice house, nice cars, and nice job. The only thing extraordinary in your life is Camille and that's partially due to her godfather's influence," he said with a chuckle. "While you may be content, you aren't really happy. You play everything safe and you hold yourself back."

"How so?" she asked, playing along but so far not persuaded by anything he had said.

He turned to look back at her. His mouth was set in a grim line.

"Why don't you have another baby?"

Julienne blinked in surprise.

"I know Greg wants another but he says you won't. Why not?"

"Well, look at you and Greg being chatty," Julienne deflected.

Daniel waited.

"We have Camille," she stated.

"And she's amazing, so why not make another amazing human?"

"We are happy with the way things are now. We can provide for her. We..."

Daniel was shaking his head.

"You aren't happy. You are playing it safe; you're scared maybe, but you aren't happy and neither is Greg."

Julienne didn't answer. She sat straight up so she was even with Daniel.

Daniel kept going.

"Why are you a teacher?"

"What's wrong with being a teacher? It's a noble profession."

"Of course, it is," Daniel affirmed, "for those who are called to be a teacher. You are just doing it to be on the same schedule as Camille. You are just doing it to play it safe. There is no joy in your face when you talk about your school, your students. Why aren't you writing?"

Julienne just shook her head.

"Jules, it's Houston. Go write for the *Chronicle*. Freelance till you find a gig at a publication that works for you. Be yourself. Be a writer. You are so bottled up trying to do everything just so; I'm surprised you don't explode."

Julienne stood up. Daniel stood, too.

"Is it hard to hear? Well, welcome to the club. For years you have been berating me and offering opinions on my life. Turnabout is fair play. If you get to comment, so do I."

Julienne started to walk away. Daniel grabbed her wrist.

"The Jules I knew was going to conquer the world. She was full of life and fearless when she headed off to college, but the Jules I see now is just wasting her time. The only time I see a glimpse of you is in your little girl. Where is that Jules?"

Julienne took a ragged breath. She turned back to face Daniel, and dammit, one lone tear had escaped.

"You are right. I always give my opinion on your life. This," she looked down at his hand on her wrist, "this is a lot. I'm going back up to the cabin to take a shower."

Daniel just stared at her. He reached up and wiped the tear away with his thumb.

"Okay, Jules," he said as he let go.

She stopped at their spot to grab her towel and slip on her flip-flops. Then she walked back to the cabin by herself.

CHAPTER 8

Julienne rinsed off in the outdoor shower to get all the sand off of her. The boards encasing the shower were old and worn from the wind and the sun; a mottled grey color showed their age and sturdiness. The water was warm and the pressure was just enough to get the sand off her body. Ever since she was a little girl Julienne had always got a kick out of rinsing off in the outdoor shower.

She wrapped the towel around her and headed upstairs to the cabin. Then she treated herself to a long soak in the tub. She found some bath salts to add to the water. The eucalyptus smell added to the relaxation of the soak. At home, she was always rushing to get through her showers because Camille, Greg, or even the dog always needed something. Once out of the tub she wrapped her hair in a towel and wrapped herself in an old robe that had always lived at the cabin. Noticing her tan lines from the day on the beach, Julienne lathered herself up in lotion. She took a breath. She felt clean and relaxed.

Julienne looked down at her phone on the counter to check the time and the smiling face of her daughter looked back at her. Camille had her brown eyes and dark hair. Her hair was in pigtails and her cheeks were red from playing that day. Camille was the best part of Julienne.

She wondered how her daughter was at this moment. If she had to guess, she was tuckered out from a day of fishing. Camille was six and a miniature version of Julienne, except nothing tragic had occurred to make her silent. She never stopped talking. To Julienne, Camille's birth after the initial miscarriage was still a miracle.

She remembered that day. The nurse had placed seven pounds, eleven ounces of pure joy in her arms. Camille had arrived safe and sound with no problems at all. Greg could not stop beaming. Her aunt and uncle were taking pictures from every angle. And Julienne, well, she just felt relieved.

It felt like she had held her breath for nine months. She kept waiting for something to go wrong, but the universe had worked in her favor this time. She was tired but happy. Now, Julienne just needed Daniel to be there. Then her day would be complete.

Every time the door to her pale green hospital room opened, Julienne looked up in anticipation, but it was always a nurse, never Daniel. Greg had left several messages but Daniel had not responded. In the back of her mind, Julienne wondered what was wrong.

Daniel's divorce was final two months ago. She and Greg had him over to the house for a divorce dinner; plus, Greg needed help with the baby's crib. When Daniel left their house that night, they both knew he was headed to a bar. When Julienne called him the next day, a girl answered his phone.

Drinking and one-night stands had become Daniel's standard operating procedure. But he had been good to

Julienne. Daniel accompanied her to the doctor on two occasions when Greg was out of town. Daniel would always hold her hand while Julienne would wait with bated breath until she heard the heartbeat. Then Daniel would give her hand a squeeze and Julienne would squeeze right back. She and Greg had opted not to find out the gender of the baby, but Daniel always predicted Julienne was having a girl.

Daniel painted the nursery a buttery yellow and then surprised Julienne with a mural of the night sky on the ceiling. Her daughter had a custom Daniel Hawk painting to gaze at to her heart's content.

Greg wanted to ask his sister to be the baby's godmother and Julienne agreed. She was going to ask Daniel to be the godfather, but first he had to show up to meet the baby.

Her aunt and uncle took Greg to get some food. Julienne had gone into labor that morning and now it was the afternoon and none of them had remembered to eat. Julienne wasn't hungry. Instead, she took in the quiet and closed her eyes.

When she opened them, Daniel was there. His back was to her. His eyes were on the baby. He had on a plaid shirt, jeans, and his hair hung down just a little over his collar. Julienne smiled. Now her day was complete.

"Daniel," she whispered.

He turned around, "Hey, beautiful."

Daniel took the two steps necessary to sit in the chair next to her bed. Julienne noticed the circles under his eyes. With the blue plaid on today, his eyes looked dark blue. She started to ask but then decided to leave it alone. Daniel grabbed her hand.

"What do you think?" she asked.

"She is beautiful, just like her mother," Daniel said, running his thumb up and down the top of her hand.

"Her name is Camille Rayne," Julienne declared.

Daniel's eyebrows shot up, "Rayne for Rainier?"

Julienne nodded her head.

"It's perfect," Daniel said. "I bet your parents–I bet they love that," he said, gesturing up.

Julienne smiled. She squeezed his hand.

"I'm glad you're here."

"Where else would I be?" Daniel asked.

Julienne shrugged her shoulders but held on to his hand.

"Now, I hear when baby sleeps, so does mom, so close your eyes."

Julienne pointed to her forehead. Daniel obliged with a kiss. She closed her eyes and drifted off to sleep with Daniel holding her hand.

When she woke, Daniel was gone. Greg had returned, and the baby was stirring.

Holding Camille, Julienne realized she had forgotten to ask Daniel to be the godfather. But of course, she would ask, and she knew he would say yes.

Daniel had said yes to being Camille's godfather, but bringing him to the beach was more like a kidnapping. She had really given Daniel no choice.

Julienne shook her head at herself for this beach plan. She continued to replay what Daniel had said back at the beach about her life. Daniel was half right; her life on paper would have appeared perfect, but in the rare moments when Julienne had a moment to write in her journal, the word lonely appeared more than once.

Julienne took her hair down from the towel and decided to let it air dry. She changed into shorts and a shirt. Then she grabbed her phone and went to sit outside on the deck and call her daughter.

While Camille was regaling her with every detail of her fishing adventures, Daniel came up the stairs. He gave her a wink and went inside. Ten minutes later, Camille was still chattering away and Daniel came out freshly showered in shorts and a tee. He held up Julienne's car keys and was mouthing something Julienne could not make out.

All Julienne could think was oh shit, Daniel is trying to leave. This wasn't part of the plan. Daniel started downstairs. Julienne was holding her hand out trying to stop him. He continued down the stairs.

Julienne got up to follow him, while trying to end her conversation with her daughter.

"That's great," she heard herself say into the phone. "Mommy has to go, but you can tell me more tomorrow."

Daniel was halfway down the stairs.

"Of course, I miss you," Julienne answered her daughter. "Mommy loves you more than the moon and the stars."

Daniel looked up at that comment. He was at the bottom of the stairs now.

Julienne was tiptoeing down the stairs since she had no shoes on her feet.

"Yes, baby, I will talk to you tomorrow. Okay, au revoir."

Camille only knew a few French words but the ones she did know she insisted on using every chance she got; hence the au revoir. Julienne ended the conversation just as she reached the bottom of the stairs.

Daniel was getting in the driver's side.

"Um, hello," Julienne stammered.

Daniel looked up. He was standing by her car with the driver's side door open.

"Oh, are you talking to me?"

Julienne nodded.

Daniel laughed.

"I thought you were still on the phone with Camille."

Julienne crossed her arms and asked, "Daniel, where do you think you are going?"

Daniel laughed again. Julienne shifted her weight on the concrete.

"To get the tacos, silly. Did you want to ride?"

"The tacos," Julienne repeated, scrunching up her nose.

Daniel stepped out from behind the door and took a step towards Julienne.

"Yes, Jules, the tacos. I told you that upstairs. Fish tacos? From our favorite taco stand?"

Julienne still stood there processing. Daniel had tried to mouth something to her. Had he really said tacos? Her first thought had been departure, not dinner.

Julienne let her arms fall to her sides.

"Is that what you were saying when I was on the phone with Camille?"

"Jules," Daniel shook his head. "Did you get too much sun today? What's so hard to understand about me going to get us some food?"

"I, well, I just thought," Julienne stammered. "Never mind."

"You sure?" Daniel continued.

Julienne nodded her head, still processing that he wasn't trying to leave, just trying to feed them.

"Okay," Daniel said and started to get back in the car.

Julienne shouted, "Wait!"

Daniel stopped.

She walked over to where he was and put out her hand.

"You can't drive, neighbor. You just got a DUI."

Daniel looked down at the keys in his hand. Then he looked back up to Jules.

"I guess you're right," Daniel sighed. "But you can't drive, either, Jules. You don't have on any shoes."

Julienne looked down at her feet. She had no shoes. Daniel, for the time being, had no license. All she could do was look up and smile.

"Okay, Jules," Daniel said, handing her the keys. "Go put some shoes on so we can get some food. And we are also making a stop for some nail polish."

Julienne raised her eyebrows.

"Those toes need some help," Daniel smirked.

Julienne didn't look down because she knew he was right. Her toenails needed some color.

As she started back up the stairs, she called over her shoulder, "Oh really, so maybe you try out some of those paint skills on my toes tonight."

"Done," Daniel agreed.

An hour later with their stomachs full, they were spread out on the sofa watching *Guys and Dolls* for the thousandth time.

Julienne had put up a mild protest, but this was Daniel's favorite musical and somehow a copy of it was at the cabin. In exchange for making Julienne watch it, Daniel produced a bottle of red nail polish.

"Can I make one request?" Julienne asked.

Daniel pointed to her feet resting on a pillow on his lap.

"Um, Jules, I think you already did."

Julienned poked him with her right foot and proceeded with her demand.

"Can you please not say all of Marlon Brando's lines?'

Daniel shook his head.

"I do not do that, Jules."

Julienne poked him again.

"Yes, you do, Sky Masterson. It's no fun watching when you say and attempt to sing all his parts."

Daniel grabbed both her feet in a preemptive effort not to be poked again and declared, "Jules, I'm hurt. I just enjoy the movie. So maybe my enthusiasm gets a little carried away, but I mean, come one."

"A little carried away," Julienne countered. "Dude, you dressed up as Sky Masterson three years in a row for Halloween."

"First of all, I rock some pinstripes and a fedora. Second, I seem to remember you matching me one year."

Julienne shook her head.

"Yea, I wanted to be a hot box girl, but you made me dress up as Jean Simmons, all buttoned up in her good girl, missionary outfit."

"Jules, Sky and Sarah go together," Daniel countered. "And no way was I taking you out in Houston in a hot box girl outfit. I would have been fighting boys all night."

Julienne laughed. She had really wanted to be a hot box girl. In the movie, they wore black lace pin-up girl outfits with the cinched-in waist and fishnet stockings. Daniel had absolutely refused.

"But back to my original request," Julienne persisted.

"Fine," Daniel acquiesced. "I will be quiet."

Instead of saying all the lines, Daniel focused on her feet. First, he rubbed them with lotion. Then, with care and precision, he painted her toes with a blood-red polish.

Julienne leaned back and enjoyed the foot rub and the musical.

Daniel even caught her humming along when Jean Simmons' character sang "If I were a bell."

"I knew it," he said.

"Knew what," Julienne answered.

"I knew you secretly wanted to be Sarah Brown."

"And why would I want to be her?" Julienne played along as Daniel finished painting her toes.

"Because she ends up with me," Daniel grinned.

Julienne shook her head.

"You mean she ends up with Sky Masterson."

"You know what I mean," Daniel said as he put the top back on the nail polish. "Your toes are much improved."

Julienne lifted her right leg to see the finished product.

"They look nice," she commented. "I don't usually go for red."

"But I do," Daniel countered. "Men like red toes, Jules."

Julienne picked up the bottle from the coffee table to see the actual name. When she read it, she sat straight up.

"Daniel James Hawk," she exclaimed, using his full name while hitting him with the bottle.

Daniel retreated to the far side of the sofa, asking "What?"

"You," she held up the bottle, "You painted my toes a color named 'Size Matters.'"

Daniel shook his head no.

"Jules, I painted your toes red."

Julienne threw the bottle at him.

"Look at the label," Julienne demanded.

Daniel flipped over the bottle and burst out laughing.

"Holy Shit, Jules. It's really called Size Matters."

Julienne put her head in her hands.

"What's the big deal? I just picked out a red nail polish. Who cares what the name is?"

Julienne looked up at Daniel.

"I care," she declared. "My toes, my toes feel dirty now."

"Jules, live a little. And your toes, they are sexy no matter what the name is and besides, I mean the name isn't wrong...size does matter."

Julienne put her head back in her hands.

"Come on, Jules," Daniel coaxed. "Your toes look pretty. Come sit by me. Marlon is about to sing 'Luck be a Lady.'"

Julienne looked up and then looked at her toes, which were propped up on the coffee table.

"They do look pretty," she agreed.

Then she scooted closer to Daniel. He put his arm around her. She laid her head on his shoulder. Just as Marlon began to sing, she said in a whisper, "You tell no one the name of this polish."

Daniel whispered back, "Or else..."

"Or else I tell everyone you cried at the last Nicholas Sparks novel."

Daniel without hesitation said, "It's a deal."

Julienne relaxed and fell asleep before the movie was over. When she woke up her head was still on Daniel's shoulder, but at some point, he had stretched out on the sofa and Julienne was lying on top of him. His hand was on the small of her back. Her hand was on his other shoulder. He was warm, and lying there was–to her surprise–comfortable.

She typically did not like to snuggle, but this wasn't snuggling. This was just falling asleep on her neighbor. She pushed herself up to see the time on the cable box. It was a little after three.

Julienne thought, I should get up and go to bed. She wrinkled her nose at the thought of should. Her whole life, she had always done what she should do. What a person should do versus what they wanted to do or needed to do; well, those things did not always align.

Daniel sighed in his sleep. Julienne pushed his hair back from his eyes. There was just enough moonlight streaming in through the sliding glass doors for Julienne to see his face. The bruises were healing. She traced his jaw. He was so familiar to her, yet sometimes–like when she picked him up from jail–she did not know him at all.

She swung her leg over and stood up from the sofa. Before she could take a step, Daniel circled her wrist with his left hand.

With his eyes still closed, he said, "Don't go."

Julienne bent down and gave him a forehead kiss. And then she took that step towards the bedroom.

Daniel let go of her wrist, saying, "The companionship of a doll is a pleasant thing."

Julienne kept walking but the musical quote made her smile.

"Is that what I am," she asked over her shoulder. "A doll?"

Daniel rolled over to his side, grabbing the blanket she had left behind, content to sleep on the sofa.

"Jules, you're the best doll."

Julienne smiled and crawled into bed.

CHAPTER 9

Julienne opened one eye the next morning to a bedroom full of sunshine. She grabbed her phone to check the time: 10 a.m. Julienne couldn't remember the last time she slept that late. She stretched out in the iron bed and thought she could roll over and go back to sleep, but the smell of coffee from the kitchen caught her attention.

She grabbed her phone and got up. This time she paid attention to the whole screen and saw three missed calls from Greg.

"Oops," she thought. "I bet he doesn't think I am a very good doll."

Julienne grinned at herself and then shook her head. Greg was not happy, and she needed to call him back and get the conversation over with, but first she needed coffee.

The coffee pot was full, but Daniel was not in the cabin. She first looked out to check on her car, which was still parked right where they left it. She shrugged. Daniel would turn up. She fixed her coffee with plenty of creamer and went to sit outside on the deck.

She took the first sip and then called her husband. She

put the phone on speaker and leaned back in the chair. A few people were walking along the shore. The sand was freshly grated thanks to Galveston county beach patrol. A breeze was blowing and the waves were crashing. It was almost hypnotic.

Greg answered on the third ring.

"Julienne, what the hell?"

"Well, good morning to you, too," Julienne answered.

"Don't be flippant. I am not in the mood."

Julienne sat up a little straighter.

"Well, neither am I, Greg, neither am I."

A moment passed and then another. Neither said a word. It was a phone standoff. Julienne leaned back again in the chair and pulled her knees up to her chest. She could sit here all day. Her view was pleasant; plus, she had a fresh cup of coffee.

Finally, Greg said, "Well..."

"Well, what?"

"Well, what do you have to say for yourself?"

"Excuse me?"

Julienne wished her voice had not gotten higher on the word me. It showed her annoyance and she wanted to remain calm during this conversation.

"Julienne, I called three times. Do you want to tell me what is going on that you cannot answer the phone?"

"I was sleeping," Julienne said, each word in her teacher voice.

Greg scoffed.

Julienne continued, "That's right Greg: sleeping. This is my one week off. Camille is with my aunt and uncle and you are out of town, so yes, God forbid, I slept late this morning."

"You never sleep late."

Julienne wondered where Greg was having this phone call. Had he stepped out into the hallway? Was he using someone's office? She could picture him in his usual color scheme of grey and navy. His hair would be brushed back. His face clean-shaven. He represented the firm well, which is why they sent him out so much. He looked the part and he was smart enough yet affable enough to sell the accounting firm to a wide array of corporate clients.

"No, I am never able to sleep late," Julienne answered, thinking: I let the dog out. I make your breakfast. I feed and dress our daughter. I am a tired working mom.

"Look, I'm sorry I missed your calls and I'm sorry if you were worried but I'm fine. Camille's fine. The dog is fine. The neighbor has been checking on him."

Julienne took another sip of coffee, hoping that answer would satisfy Greg.

"Great, the neighbor," Greg said, almost in a whisper.

"What?"

"Just what I need–another neighbor in my life," Greg answered.

"You are being ridiculous," Julienne said in return just as she heard footsteps on the stairs. Daniel had a huge smile on his face. He started to say something, but Julienne put a finger to her lips, hoping he would stay silent.

"Am I, Julienne? Am I?" Greg questioned back.

Daniel nodded at the sound of Greg's voice. He gave her shoulder a squeeze and went inside the cabin. She was glad to see him up and smiling today.

"You're right," Greg continued. "You deserve this week. I envisioned the spa and yes, even you sleeping late, but in our bed in our home–not at the beach with your neighbor."

"Well, being here is good for me."

Greg made another noise somewhere between a grunt and a laugh.

"And it's good for him, so I'm so sorry it doesn't fit your vision."

"When are you coming home?"

Julienne didn't respond right away.

"I don't know," she admitted.

"That's not good enough," Greg said, his voice getting louder.

"Well, that's all I have."

"You need to come home," Greg said again in the loud voice.

"No," Julienne answered.

"Excuse me?"

"I said no."

Julienne scanned the beach again. A dog was playing fetch with its owner. She liked it here. They did not come here enough. Greg was not really a beach person, but she was. She was staying. She might have first thought to come to the beach for Daniel, but she was staying for herself.

"You are gone till Friday. Camille doesn't get back till Saturday, so no, I don't need to come home. There is nothing for me to come home to. This is my week."

"So, you are staying there," Greg asked again, as if he needed further confirmation.

"Yes."

"With him?"

"Yes."

"I am not okay with this, Julienne. I thought you were

done rescuing him."

"That's not what I am doing."

And Julienne resented Greg in that moment. It felt good to make a decision for herself. Maybe she should go home, but what she wanted was to stay the rest of the week at the beach.

"Fine," Greg said, and Julienne could sense another hang-up was coming.

"Why did you tell Daniel you wanted another baby?"

"What?" Greg replied. "Where did that come from?"

"You act like he is the enemy here, but clearly he is your friend too; you told him you wanted another baby."

Julienne knew she had flipped the script, but Daniel's words from yesterday were still very much on her mind.

"Because..."

"Because why?" Julienne said again in her teacher voice, waiting for a proper reply.

"Because when I can't get through to you sometimes, he can."

Julienne sat up and put her feet on the deck while she processed what Greg had just said.

"So, you were using him to get to me, to manipulate me into having a baby," Julienne said as half question, half statement.

"No, Julienne, it wasn't like that; he's my friend too. We were just having a beer, guy talk."

"Oh, now he's your friend; I can't keep up."

"Julienne, just–we will talk about this when you get home; whenever that is," Greg said with the fight gone out of his voice.

Julienne had no response; no good one anyway, so she hung up this time.

She took another sip of coffee. She looked back through the sliding glass doors and saw Daniel making himself busy in the kitchen. She wondered how much of that he heard. She wondered how much she would have to explain.

Being at the beach was almost like being kids again when they lived next door to each other and pretty much spent all their time together.

Funny, right now she almost had too much access to Daniel, but there had been a time when he had all but disappeared from her life. Julienne had been immersed in motherhood; Greg in work.

And then one night Julienne was rinsing the dishes from dinner and loading the dishwasher. It was 9:00 p.m. on a Tuesday. Two-year-old Camille had been bathed, read a story, and put to bed. Greg was in the bedroom answering work e-mail and watching some form of a game.

Julienne was opposed to a television in the bedroom. She thought their bedroom should be a sanctuary, a place for peaceful sleep and, of course, quality time together. The 46" flat-screen TV on the wall opposite their bed was evidence she had lost that battle with Greg. Daniel agreed with her, but she wasn't married to Daniel.

She had fallen into the routine of waiting for Greg to fall asleep, then creeping in to turn off the TV and go to bed.

Julienne was staring out the kitchen window above the sink, thinking about everything and nothing all at the same time. Greg wanted to consider having another child. Julienne did not. She felt they would be pushing their luck. Julienne wanted a pedicure. Greg wanted shrimp tomorrow for dinner, which meant a trip to the market. The trivial and the serious mixed together in her thoughts.

Her hair was pulled up in a ponytail. She had no time to put on makeup that day, so the circles under her eyes from allergies and lack of sleep were prevalent. She had on a soft V-neck grey shirt and her favorite worn-out pair of jeans with flip-flops. She wore her "J" necklace Daniel had given her when she was 21; she never took that off.

Robert Downey Jr's song "Broken" was playing from the CD player tucked away in the corner. Julienne liked the sound of his voice:

In love with a broken heart
Think I leave today, I cover it all this way
You fell in love with a broken heart
Every earthly breath, a lifeless testimony
In love with a broken heart

Julienne hummed along and thought about her own broken heart when her parents died, when her dog died, when she miscarried. Julienne was familiar with a broken heart.

What brought Julienne out of her reverie was a knock on her back door. She looked over to see Daniel grinning at her through the window. She dropped the plate in her hand, which clattered loudly against the steel. She took a moment to process he was actually at her house. Julienne saw Daniel so seldom these days. Her life was motherhood and going back to school to obtain her teaching certificate. His life was, well, she wasn't sure.

Daniel just stood there smiling and Julienne dried her hands on a dishtowel and went to unlock the door.

As she opened the door, she asked, "What are you doing..."

Her question was interrupted by Daniel holding up two Dairy Queen blizzards.

Julienne squealed and gave Daniel a hug. He just held on to the blizzards and kissed her on the side of her neck.

"I like when your hair is up, Jules," Daniel declared. "The tattoo still works for you."

Julienne ushered him to the kitchen table where she quickly dug into her treat. Julienne savored the first bite of ice cream and Reese's peanut butter cups. This was her absolute favorite and Daniel knew it.

"You know, this is the last thing I need right now," she said to Daniel.

Daniel was digging into his, which he always got with butterfingers.

"Oh, Jules," Daniel sighed. "Need? Want?" he shrugged his shoulders. "You deserve it."

"Right," Julienne said with a laugh and a kick at his feet under the table and continued to eat.

"Is my goddaughter asleep?" Daniel asked.

Julienne nodded in affirmation and continued to eat.

"Greg?" Daniel asked.

"In the bedroom watching sports," Julienne replied.

They continued eating their treats. Daniel looked okay. Julienne could tell when she hugged him, he wasn't too skinny. His hair was long. He appeared tired, but then again, so did she. His eyes were clear, though, and that was good. His eyes looked clear and were a shade of light blue tonight against his white tee.

"You should wear more green," Julienne declared.

Daniel nodded his head, "Duly noted."

"You know I like..."

"Green eyes," Daniel finished for her. "This I know. Your dad had green eyes."

Julienne smiled and sat back in her chair. She had missed the comfortableness of their friendship. That's what happens when you have been friends since the third grade–most things you already know, like Julienne favored green eyes.

"So, is this a bribe?" Julienne said, half teasing, half not. "Do you need something?"

Daniel shook his head and put his hand over his heart.

"That hurts, Jules. I have absolutely no hidden agenda at all."

"Okay," Julienne said as she licked her spoon of the last remaining remnants of her blizzard.

"I just missed you," Daniel said, looking down. "And I thought you deserved a treat."

They sat for a moment. Julienne squeezed his hand and said, "Thank you, neighbor."

Daniel returned the squeeze.

"You're welcome, Jules."

That night Julienne slept well. Her stomach was full, and her friend seemed to be doing well.

The next morning, her phone vibrated at 5:15. She reached for her phone on the nightstand immediately, thinking something must be wrong.

The text read: Put on your running shoes. Meet me outside.

Julienne lay there in disbelief. Greg let out a snore. She wanted to roll over and go back to sleep. Her phone vibrated again.

The second text read: NOW

Julienne slipped out of bed, trying to be quiet. In the bathroom she brushed her teeth and dressed as she had been instructed. She went out the front door and on her sidewalk was Daniel in shorts and running shoes.

Julienne just stared. She couldn't remember the last time she saw Daniel in shorts. He always wore jeans. As a result, his legs were super pale. If she was more awake, she might have laughed.

Walking towards him, she asked, "What are you doing?"

Daniel grinned, "We need to run off those blizzards from last night."

Julienne just shook her head, commenting, "You are crazy."

"Well, that's not news," Daniel chuckled. Then he nudged her forward.

"What," Julienne asked, "no stretching?"

"That's called procrastination," Daniel replied with a wink. "Let's go."

They ran two miles in the early morning humidity of Houston, Texas. Julienne was sure she was going to die, or at the very least throw-up. Pushing a stroller clearly was not enough to maintain physical fitness.

When they were done, Daniel gave her a quick hug and headed to his truck.

"You aren't coming inside?" Julienne asked.

"No," Daniel called over his shoulder. "Busy day."

Julienne just stood there and watched Daniel drive off. He waved. She concentrated on breathing. Then she turned to go inside her house. The coffee had started automatically. Julienne could hear the water in the shower running, so Greg was up. Camille wouldn't wake up till closer to 7:00. Julienne was still processing how her morning had started. Then she began making breakfast. Running had left her hungry.

This became their pattern over the next few weeks, which then became months. Daniel would show up with their treats on Tuesday nights, and then they would run on Wednesday mornings.

Sometimes he would get there in time to read Camille a bedtime story and tuck her into bed. This always made the toddler and her mother happy.

Greg stayed out their way. He referred to it as their BFF time.

Daniel told her about the classes he was teaching at the art institute and the side projects he was working on for his growing clientele, still murals and now some custom portraits. Julienne told him about becoming certified to teach. They caught up on each other's lives and settled back into the easy rhythm of their friendship.

Julienne figured out Daniel went to group therapy on Tuesday nights; hence the clear eyes. He never talked about it. She never asked.

Julienne appreciated that he showed up at her back door every Tuesday night and her front door every Wednesday morning.

Julienne looked forward to it, expected it, and even began to accept it as a given.

Julienne had her neighbor Daniel back. It was the first time she felt like he was okay since the divorce. It had been a long three years.

And that was it. The moment she relaxed and exhaled, that was the week he did not show up.

But Daniel was here now, and Julienne had dug her

heels in the sand with Greg. They were at the beach and they were staying through the end of the week.

Julienne decided she needed more coffee and went inside to join Daniel. He was busy making brunch. She did not offer any information about her conversation with Greg. Daniel did not ask.

They spent the afternoon on the deck. Julienne put her yellow bathing suit back on and lay out to read. Daniel set himself up in the far corner of the deck and spent the whole time sketching.

Sometimes they talked. Most of the time they didn't. For Julienne it was a do-nothing day and she reveled in it. Camille called her late that afternoon to once again report on her fishing adventures. With another long protracted good-bye, Camille took her time getting off the phone with her mother.

When Julienne was done, she announced to Daniel, "Time to go in. I am done for the day."

Daniel continued to sketch.

"I am not far behind you. I am just finishing this up."

"Can I see?" Julienne asked, already knowing the answer.

Daniel looked up at her with a smirk.

"No, not until it's done," which was his usual response.

Julienne slid open the glass door, but Daniel interrupted her progress with a request.

"Hey, Jules, let's go out to eat tonight."

Julienne looked over her shoulder. Her first response was they should stay in and eat the food she bought; plus, she did not have anything to wear. But when she thought about it, going to eat would be fun and they had the rest of the week to eat the food she bought.

Julienne looked over her shoulder and shrugged, "Sure, why not?"

CHAPTER 10

In the end Julienne found a sundress in the back of the closet that she must have left behind years ago. It was a cream-colored cotton dress trimmed in lace that felt soft on her suntanned skin. She pulled her hair back in a messy bun, swiped on some mascara and lip gloss, and was ready to go.

They went to a restaurant on the bayside where the food was fried and the beer was cold. They laughed through dinner, and when the waitress asked them if they had room for dessert, Julienne's response was, "Sure, why not."

They split a piece of key lime pie, which was Julienne's favorite to eat at the beach probably because that was one of the few memories she had of her parents. She remembered being at the beach and eating key lime pie with her dad when she was little. She remembered sitting on his lap, one giant piece of pie, and two spoons. She remembered being happy.

On their way out of the restaurant, the jukebox was playing an Earl Thomas Conley song. The song reminded her of the one time she and Daniel had gotten into a fight. Dinner had been relaxing, but in the car ride her mind wandered back to that memory.

Julienne remembered she was in the middle of icing cupcakes when her phone rang. It was Friday evening. It had been a long week. Julienne was still getting used to being a teacher. She enjoyed the interactions with her students. She was still learning how to make high school English something students at the very least did not despise. The best part of her day was leaving at 3 p.m. to go pick up her daughter at preschool. The worst part of her day was staying up late grading essays after Camille went to sleep.

Tomorrow they were hosting a backyard birthday party for their four-year-old replete with a jump-jump and plenty of sugar for the children and the adults to consume. Right now, she had four dozen cupcakes to ice and she was questioning her sanity in making them herself instead of ordering from the bakery.

Her phone was singing "Let It Be Me" by Ray LaMontagne so she knew it was Daniel. He had programmed that ringtone for himself, and they both knew why.

Julienne wiped off her hands and answered, "Yes."

"Hey, Jules," Daniel answered back.

"What's up," Julienne asked.

"I was calling about Camille's party tomorrow."

Julienne took a quick breath and said, "Do not tell me you are not coming. That little girl will be so disappointed."

And so will I, Julienne thought.

"No, silly," Daniel said. "Pessimistic, much?"

Julienne put the phone on speaker and resumed icing

the cupcakes.

"Sorry, I just have a lot to do between now and then. I'm counting on you being there."

"Of course," Daniel said, even though they both knew he was better at the spontaneous visits versus the planned ones. Those were the ones he tended to blow off. The old Daniel wouldn't have blown off any plans with Julienne, but no one stays the same. Silence ensued as Julienne iced yet another cupcake.

Julienne broke the moment of silence by saying, "So."

"Right, so I was wondering if I could bring someone tomorrow."

"Really," Julienne's voice rose on the two-syllable word.

"Yes, really," Daniel countered. "Don't sound so surprised, or was that dismay?"

"I didn't know you were seeing anyone, like actually dating."

"I date," Daniel stated.

"No, you don't," Julienne responded without hesitation.

"What is it I do, Jules?" Daniel asked.

"Well, to put it nicely," Julienne said, continuing her work with the cupcakes, "you have one-night stands. You, you love 'em and leave 'em. You are like a bad country song."

"That's putting it nicely," Daniel questioned.

"Yes," Julienne retorted. "That is the nice version."

"Try putting it not so nicely," Daniel continued.

"Okay," Julienne said slowly. "You fuck lots of women."

"What?" Daniel asked.

"You heard me," Julienne responded.

"No, I don't think I did," Daniel was incredulous. "Try again."

Julienne sighed and this time louder with more confidence, she said, "Daniel, you fuck lots of women."

Daniel broke into a belly laugh. Greg chose that moment to walk into the kitchen. Julienne had decorated the kitchen around her parent's china. Her mother had chosen a classic white china with a black border and silver trim. She had accented the kitchen with pops of yellow, including a weekly purchase of yellow roses to go in a crystal vase. Greg did not see the point in buying flowers, but they made Julienne happy.

Greg shot her an inquisitive look, but she shook her head. Greg grabbed a beer and headed outside to complete his list of chores.

Julienne spoke over Daniel's laughter.

"I don't see what's so funny."

Daniel caught his breath from laughing.

"You, Jules," Daniel declared. "You are funny."

"Well, you asked," she retorted, continuing on the endless supply of cupcakes.

"Yes, I did," Daniel asked. "What are you doing right now, anyway?"

"I am icing cupcakes."

"You are so domestic," Daniel commented.

Julienne sighed again and said, "I know. What are you doing?"

"Driving to meet my date."

"The one you want to bring tomorrow?" Julienne asked.

"Yes, that one," Daniel answered. "If tonight goes well."

"I don't know," Julienne said. "Are you sure that's a good idea? It's just a few family and friends and a bunch of four-year-olds."

"Are you telling me no?"

"Of course not," Julienne said without hesitation. "When do I ever tell you no?"

Even though Daniel did not say anything, Julienne knew he was smiling because the answer was never. She never told him no, and they both knew it.

"Are you sure this is something the kind of girl you date would enjoy? A four-year-old's birthday party?"

Daniel broke into laughter again.

"Jules, you continue to make me smile," he said. "This one will love it. I promise."

"Okay," Julienne said reluctantly.

"Okay," Daniel said. "One more thing. Camille's gift is really big, so I am going to have to bring it over in pieces and put it together there. Okay, bye."

With that, the phone call ended. Julienne just shook her head.

The next day arrived with clear September skies. It was still hot in Houston but not too hot.

The backyard was decorated in purple and white. Camille had insisted her dad hang the unicorn piñata first thing that morning. Camille's favorite color was purple and her favorite animal was a unicorn, which explained the party theme.

Camila had on a purple dress with ruffles. She had a pile of curls on top of her head with a princess crown. She had wanted Julienne to wear purple, too, but Julienne had pointed out only the birthday girl should be in the birthday colors. Instead, Julienne had on a cobalt blue sundress with wedges for a little height. If she was being honest with herself, she put that dress on today because Daniel had commented that she should wear more blue. He liked her dark hair against any shade of blue; supposedly he was going to paint her in a blue dress one day.

Julienne did not think blue did anything for her brown eyes, but if she wanted Daniel to wear more green, she would acquiesce and wear more blue.

Her aunt and uncle showed up early to help. As her uncle got older, Julienne always imagined how her dad would look. The brothers had the same features with a slightly crooked nose, the same wavy hair. The only difference was her uncle's brown eyes. Her father's had been green. Her uncle was the closest thing she had to a dad, though, and she appreciated him now more than ever. She gave him a hug before he joined Greg.

The men headed straight to the grill. Her aunt helped in the kitchen. Camille bounced back and forth, eager for her party to begin.

People started showing up at 1:00 on the dot. By 2:00 four-year-olds were bouncing away on the jump-jump. Daniel still had not arrived. Julienne was waiting on him to do the cake and presents.

At 2:30 Greg supervised the destruction of the piñata, and Julienne went inside to grab her phone and call Daniel. It went straight to voicemail. Julienne figured his date went really well or really bad last night. Either way, to put it in preschool language, Daniel was not making good choices.

Julienne went back outside. Greg shot her a look. She shrugged her shoulders. It was time for cupcakes. They sang happy birthday, loud and out of tune. Camille blew out her candles. All the little ones picked out cupcakes and so did the adults. The party was experiencing a quiet lull while everyone ate their desserts.

Greg had the radio playing and Julienne could just hear the opening chords of "Brown Eyed Girl." Her father had sung this song to her. It was one of her favorite memories of her dad.

Camille made eye contact with her mother and Julienne smiled from ear to ear. It warmed Julienne's heart knowing her own little brown-eyed girl recognized the song as well. It was their theme song.

At that moment, Daniel walked into the party, in reality more like stumbled.

Camille squealed, "Godfather."

She jumped from her seat and ran to him. Daniel scooped her up and twirled her around. All you could see was a flurry of purple in the air.

"My parrain," she used the French word for godfather. "I am so glad you are here."

She put a chubby little hand on each of his cheeks and gave him a loud kiss. Daniel maintained a lopsided grin. His hair was rumpled. His clothes were rumpled. One look told Julienne Daniel had no business being there.

"Godfather," Camille continued. "My song is playing. It's my song and mommy's. Dance," she commanded.

Daniel started to move. Camille had her hands around his neck. She giggled with the perceived fun of it all. However, watching Daniel stumble with her daughter was painful for Julienne. Greg came to stand by her. His arms were folded across his chest. His expression matched her thoughts.

When Daniel bumped into the table with the gifts,

Julienne nudged Greg forward.

"Okay, Dad's turn to dance with the birthday girl," Greg announced as he held his arms out and Daniel handed Camille over.

Greg continued the dance and Daniel continued his stumbling towards Julienne.

"Jules," he said, holding his arms out for a hug.

Julienne took his right hand and began to drag him inside. They passed her aunt, who gave her a look. She wasn't sure if she saw disapproval or sympathy from her aunt.

"Jules, you're being so domineering. I like it."

Julienne did not answer until she had him in her bedroom with the door shut. Then Julienne let go of his hand and turned to face him.

"I like your blue dress," Daniel said in a low voice.

"Don't," Julienne said. "What are you doing?"

"Isn't it obvious," Daniel said. "I came to the party."

"She's four, Daniel," Julienne said.

"I know," Daniel answered back.

"It's my daughter's fourth birthday. You can't show up like this."

"Like what?" Daniel asked, standing up straighter.

"Don't be obtuse," Julienne responded with a roll of her eyes.

"Jules," Daniel reverted back to the nickname and dragged the one syllable out as he took a step closer to her. "Jules, are we in a fight? What are we fighting about?"

"You have to be fucking kidding me," Julienne exclaimed, heading to the bathroom.

"Jules, you said the 'f' word," Daniel said in disbelief. "I like it when you curse."

Julienne came back with two aspirin and a glass of water. She shoved both at Daniel. He looked at what she was offering and then chose compliance. He took the aspirin.

"This is my daughter's day," Julienne said firmly. "This is not about you. Whatever it is this time, I don't have time for it."

She pulled the covers back on the bed.

"Am I going to bed?" Daniel asked.

"Yes," Julienne replied. "I'm pretty sure you are still drunk, and I need you to sleep it off while I go deal with the rest of the party."

"Okay," Daniel said, kicking off his shoes and getting into bed. Julienne pulled up the covers and turned to leave.

"Jules," Daniel said.

"Yes," she answered without turning around.

"I'm sorry."

"I know you are," she said with her back still to him. "But this is getting old. You're like fucking Humpty Dumpty, and I'm tired of putting you back together every time."

Julienne took another step.

"I'll do better," Daniel said in a quiet voice.

"Just sleep," Julienne replied as she flipped the light switch and rejoined the party.

Later Julienne would discover Daniel had been out with Tara. Daniel thought they were getting back together, but instead she chose a very public restaurant to let him know she was getting married. According to David, Tara left in a huff and Daniel stayed and did something he knew how to do well: get drunk.

Julienne thought it was sweet David felt the need to tell

her why Daniel was in such a state on Camille's birthday. He wanted to make sure Julienne understood and didn't hold a grudge. Of course, Julienne wouldn't hold a grudge, and David's explanation made sense in light of Daniel's behavior.

However, David told her this later and at the time, at the party, she knew nothing except Daniel showed up a mess to her daughter's party.

Julienne left Daniel in their bedroom and went back outside to supervise the opening of the presents. Camille was too caught up in the gifts to wonder where her godfather was, but Greg was not.

"He leave," he half stated, half questioned as he came up to stand by Julienne.

Julienne just shook her head.

Keeping his eyes on his daughter, Greg asked, "Julienne, where is he?"

"In the house."

Greg turned his head to stare at her and wait for further elaboration.

"Sleeping."

Greg continued to wait.

"In our bed."

Greg made a snort of disapproval and walked off. He came back with a trash bag for the remnants of the gift wrap, but he stood by her aunt this time and refused to look at Julienne.

Julienne kept busy handing out treat bags and thanking everyone as they one by one made their departures.

Later, when everyone had left, her aunt asked her how Daniel was doing.

"Oh, he's sleeping," Julienne said as she started the dishwasher.

"I know that," her aunt said. "But how is he?"

Julienne shook her head.

"I really don't know."

Her aunt patted her hand. She started to speak but then she stopped herself. Instead, she went outside to corral her husband and they left.

Camille was on the sofa watching *Beauty and the Beast*, but her eyes were drooping. Julienne knew her birthday girl would be asleep soon.

Julienne wandered outside to find Greg sitting in a lawn chair drinking a beer. Julienne sat down in the chair next to him. Greg got up without a word and disappeared into the garage. He came back and handed Julienne a beer as well. It was icy and Julienne took a long sip.

They sat and drank in silence. The remains of the party had been cleaned up. The radio was still playing. Their daughter had had a great party, but there was still her neighbor to deal with.

"Julienne," Greg said.

"I know," Julienne answered.

Greg took another sip of his beer and continued, "But to be clear."

Julienne interrupted again, "Greg, I know."

Greg stood up and took another sip of beer.

Looking down at Julienne, he said, "Get him out of our bed."

Julienne nodded.

"Deal with it or I will," Greg said and went back inside.

Julienne continued to sit and sip her beer. When the bottle grew warm, she looked at her watch. It was almost

6:00 p.m. She stood up. It was time to deal with her neighbor.

Camille was asleep on the sofa. Julienne covered her with a blanket. She could hear Greg upstairs. Julienne heated up a plate of food for Daniel and went into her bedroom.

Julienne turned on the lamp by the bed and put the food on the nightstand. Daniel was sleeping on his back with one arm behind his head. He probably needed more sleep, but it would have to be in a bed that did not belong to her and Greg.

She shook him gently, but he did not respond right away.

"Hey, sleepyhead," Julienne said, trying again.

Daniel spoke her name without opening his eyes: "Jules."

"Time to wake up," she said.

Daniel turned on his side away from her.

Julienne grabbed his shoulder.

"Daniel, it's time to wake up."

Daniel sighed.

"I brought you some food," Julienne persisted.

Daniel rolled back over. Julienne grabbed another pillow and made Daniel sit up to eat.

"Jules?" Daniel said as a question.

"Yes," she said as she grabbed the plate.

"Am I sleeping on your side of the bed?" Daniel asked. "Because your pillow smells like you."

"Yes," Julienne said, smiling in spite of herself. She handed Daniel the plate with a burger with no onions, extra pickles, just like she knew he liked it. "Now eat."

When he was done eating, Daniel made three requests.

He wanted to see Camille. He wanted to spend the night. He did not want to talk about it.

Julienne said yes to seeing Camille. Yes to spending the night, but in the guest room. Last, he could have a reprieve on talking about it tonight, but tomorrow was another day.

When Daniel woke up the little girl, Camille insisted they watch *Beauty and the Beast* from the beginning. Julienne made them popcorn while Camille pointed out the princess in the movie looked like her and her mommy.

Later, Camille insisted her parrain sleep in her room, so Daniel made a pallet on the floor. Both slept soundly.

The next morning Daniel looked better. Food and sleep had both helped. His eyes were less sunken and he was no longer stumbling. Julienne made French toast for the three most important people in her life: Her daughter, her husband, and her neighbor.

The adults were quiet, but Camille made up for it by chattering nonstop.

When everyone was done eating, Julienne announced, "Camille, say good-bye to your godfather. He has to leave."

"I do?" Daniel said as a question.

"Yep, you do," Julienne answered back.

Camille climbed up on his lap to give hugs and kisses. Greg left the kitchen without a word.

"Come on, I will walk you out," Julienne said, guiding Daniel to the front door.

"Jules, what is this," Daniel asked. "It feels like you are kicking me out."

Julienne pushed Daniel through the door and down the sidewalk. The air was balmy, but it would soon heat up. Daniel still had on his rumpled clothes from the day before. Julienne was in khaki shorts and a tee. She was walking with purpose because she needed to get this over with and then get back to her life, which today included grading papers. It did not include whatever Daniel's latest drama was.

"I am," Julienne affirmed without hesitation.

"Unfuckingbelievable," Daniel said under his breath.

Julienne stopped. They were halfway down the path which led to the sidewalk. Behind her was her house. In front of her was Daniel's truck

"Excuse me," Julienne said.

"You heard me," Daniel said, facing her on the sidewalk.

"Unfuckingbelievable, is that what you said?"

"Uh-huh."

"As in me making you leave is unfuckingbelievable?"

"Right, again," Daniel answered. At that moment a car drove by with a honk and a wave from its driver. They both ignored it.

"I will tell you what is unfuckingbelievable," Julienne said, poking him in the chest. "Showing up like that yesterday. That was un-fucking-believable," Julienne said, emphasizing each syllable.

"You told me not to disappoint her," Daniel said. "So, I came."

"That's bullshit and you know it. It's one thing for me and Greg to see you like that, but not her."

"Jules, you're overreacting," Daniel said. "She didn't know anything was wrong."

"This time," Julienne answered.

"What?" Daniel asked.

"She didn't know anything was wrong this time, but

one day she will, and I won't have it. It's hard enough for me to see you like this. I will not ever have my daughter see you like that."

"But Jules, when I explain."

"Nope, I don't care," Julienne declared.

"Of course, you do. You will never believe..."

"No, Daniel," Julienne interrupted. "You aren't listening. I do not care. I cannot do this again. Life throws you a curve ball, and you act with total disregard for yourself and those who care about you. Daniel can go and do whatever he wants because his reliable BFF Jules will always show up to restore order."

Daniel started to speak, but Julienne continued.

"Jules will show up at the Riverside. Jules will come by my house and bring me food. The cab can drop me off at Jules' house. Taking care of you is a full-time job, but I can't. I have to take care of them," Jules said, pointing at her house. "I have to take care of her."

Daniel shook his head and looked down.

"Are you even listening to me?" Julienne asked.

Daniel looked back up with tears in his eyes. In a low voice, he said, "Don't act like I never took care of you."

"I didn't say you didn't," Julienne looked directly into his watery eyes. "I know what you did for me."

"Jules," Daniel said his voice cracking. "You are being so heartless."

Julienne stepped closer to Daniel. She put her hand over his heart. She could feel the steady beat of his heart. She closed her eyes and concentrated on the constancy of that beat. Then she opened her eyes, which were full of tears now, too.

"Neighbor, you have had my heart since the third

grade, but you can't have all of it. You have to leave some for the rest of the people I love."

Daniel gulped.

"Quit saying you're sorry. Quit saying you'll do better and just do it."

Daniel nodded and put his hand over hers.

When she looked at him, she still saw the boy who befriended her. The boy who was her own personal advocate. But yesterday Julienne saw a man who was a mess, a husband who was beyond frustrated, and a little girl who was going to be disappointed. This was the reason for her actions today.

Daniel started to speak, but they both heard the front door open.

Greg said, "Julienne," at the same time Camille said, "My parrain."

Julienne stepped back, taking her hand with her. Daniel wiped his eyes. Camille stopped in front of them, dressed in a mismatched outfit of orange polka dots on top and purple with silver on the bottom. Camille was pushing her doll in her stroller.

"I thought you were leaving," Camille stated.

Daniel knelt down to talk to her.

"I am. I was just talking to your mom."

"Godfather," Camille continued. "Are you sad?"

Daniel attempted a smile but gave up.

"Well, you know I'm always sad when I leave you, princess," Daniel stated.

"I know," Camille said with complete confidence. "But you will see me again."

"Of course," Daniel said. "In fact, if it's okay with your mom and dad, I will be over again next weekend to put together your birthday present."

Daniel looked over Camille's head. Julienne didn't give a response either way.

"Promise?" Camille asked.

"I promise," Daniel said with a wink.

"Okay," Camille said. "I'm walking my dolly."

And off the little girl went down the sidewalk to the left.

Daniel stood up and went down the sidewalk to the right towards his truck.

"Did y'all break up?" Greg asked.

"Yes, I think we did," Julienne replied.

"Good."

With that one word, Greg gave her a pat on the back and took off after Camille. Daniel was getting in his truck. On one side was her family, and on the other was her family. Why was she alone in the middle? When Daniel drove off his windows were down. She heard Earl Thomas Conley singing "the hardest thing I've ever had to do." In that moment she knew how the man singing felt. That memory was not one she chose to remember, but the beach had brought up lots of memories both good and bad.

They pulled up to the cabin. Daniel walked over to the one palm tree in the yard and lit up a cigarette. Julienne went upstairs but wasn't ready to go in the cabin. She sat in her usual spot on the deck and just took in the night sky. It was an inky blue and the stars were so far away they looked like pinpricks made in construction paper with the light struggling to shine through. Julienne closed her eyes.

She heard Daniel's footsteps on the stairs. They paused beside her chair, so she was not surprised when he spoke.

"Jules, you okay?" Daniel asked.

Julienne nodded her head.

Daniel put his hand on her shoulder.

"You got quiet on the way home."

Julienne grabbed his hand.

A moment passed and Julienne said in a quiet voice, "I never pitied you."

"What?" Daniel said, looking down at her away from the night sky.

Julienne repeated her statement, "I never pitied you."

Daniel came around and knelt in front of her in the chair. He grabbed both of her hands.

"I'm not following you, Jules."

Julienne explained, "You said when we first got here, you didn't want my pity. You wanted lots of things from me but not my pity."

"Oh," was all Daniel said.

Julienne sat up straighter and continued, "I feel lots of things for you, Daniel, but never pity and you should know that."

Daniel gave her hands a squeeze and started to stand up, but Julienne pulled on his hands.

Looking eye to eye, Julienne asked, "You said you wanted lots from me. What did you mean?"

Daniel looked at their hands. Their breathing had fallen into the same rhythm as the waves.

Julienne wanted an answer though, so she kept going, "What else could you want? I'm here. You have your BFF; you have the beach. You..."

Daniel cut her off.

"You're right. Tonight, I don't want for anything. I spent the day drawing at the beach and then I took a beautiful girl out to dinner. Today was damn near perfect."

Daniel brushed some wisps of her dark hair that had escaped her bun and the wind was blowing in her face. He left his hand there on the side of her face. He maintained eye contact with her for so long she almost felt like she was in a staring contest. His eyes were dark green tonight and Julienne did not mind staring into them at all.

The waves continued to crash, the wind continued to blow, and Daniel continued to hold her gaze with his hand caressing her face and almost a smile on his lips. Julienne bit her bottom lip and the spell was broken.

Daniel shook his head and said, “Oh, Jules.”

He stood up and gave her a shoulder a squeeze. The next thing she heard was the sliding glass doors. Daniel had gone inside. Julienne continued to stare at the night sky.

CHAPTER 11

The next day Daniel wanted to go into the city of Galveston, so they did just that. They spent the morning in the antique stores and art galleries off of Post Office Street. Daniel pointed out pieces here and there that caught his eye. Julienne had fun tagging along and listening to him.

For lunch she insisted they stop in the Tremont Hotel. It was where her parents spent their wedding night, so it was a connection for Julienne.

She always loved this place, with its ornate dark wood carvings and marble floor. The historic hotel represented the grandness of Galveston from the 1880s, before the great storm hit. She always loved to stop in to eat when they came into Galveston proper from the beach. She would imagine her parents walking hand in hand across the same marble floor, young and in love.

After lunch, they hit up some of the souvenir shops on the strand. Julienne bought Camille a seashell necklace. Daniel bought fudge at the confectionary. Julienne made them go into St. Mary's church to light a candle for her parents.

She would have appreciated the church no matter what for its ornateness and continuous presence in Galveston, but it was her favorite church simply because it was where her parents had gotten married. Her dad had wanted the beach but her mom had wanted a church wedding, so they compromised and got married at a church in Galveston and had a big cookout reception on the beach with the cabin as home base.

Her uncle always described her parents dancing barefoot in the sand, Paul McCartney's "Maybe I'm Amazed" playing in the background. Her dad had picked up her mom and twirled her around and according to her uncle, her mom had thrown back her head in laughter. Her uncle always smiled telling her that memory. So of course, Julienne always kept that song in her rotation.

Then the story goes while the guests continued to eat and drink, her parents came back to a suite at the Tremont.

While she said a quick prayer, Daniel stood in the back of the church admiring the stained glass. Julienne went to join him when they saw someone come out of the confessional. Daniel watched the man walk out.

Julienne commented, "I always wanted to do it in a church."

Daniel's head whipped back around to look at Julienne. "Excuse me?"

"You heard me," Julienne smirked. "I always wanted to do it in a church."

Daniel took a step back, crossed his arms, and surveyed his friend as if seeing her for the first time.

"Naughty girl," he commented.

"What," Julienne shrugged. "I am very familiar with your sexcapades. Doing it at a church cannot be that big of a deal."

Daniel took her by the elbow to guide her out of the church. He leaned in to whisper, "Um yeah, Jules, it is. It's like guaranteeing a one-way express ticket straight to hell."

He opened the door and they descended the steps back to the sidewalk.

"No way," Julienne declared as they began the walk back to the car. "God is very aware people have sex."

Daniel pulled out a piece of fudge and offered some to Julienne. She shook her head. Before he took his own bite, he said "Not in his house, though Jules. At the very least, that's disrespectful."

Julienne winked at Daniel, stating, "I think sex in a church is hot."

Daniel just shook his head.

"You know, Jules, I have always said there isn't anything I wouldn't do for you, but I think we just found the one thing."

"Really?" Julienne questioned as they reached the car and she clicked the unlock button on her car fob.

"Yes, Jules," Daniel said as they got into the car. "I will absolutely not have sex with you in a church."

Julienne just began to laugh. It was the kind of laugh that started at the center of your stomach and worked its way up until just erupting in giggles.

Daniel just continued to stare at her. Julienne continued to laugh.

With her still laughing, he commented, "I have no idea what has gotten into you."

Julienne caught her breath and started the car.

As she reversed out of the parking spot, she answered, "It's just funny, Daniel. Like the roles are reversed. All of the sudden you are the moral compass telling me I'm going to hell."

"That's not exactly what I said..."

Julienne cut him off.

"And besides, I didn't ask you to have sex with me in a church."

"Yeah, well it's not like Greg would, Jules."

"True," Julienne agreed. "He is strictly a bedroom guy."

"So," Daniel said.

"So," Julienne said as she turned right onto the main road which would take them back to the cabin. "A girl is allowed to have fantasies."

Of course, Greg and Julienne's sex life had become pretty routine. And of course, Daniel and Julienne had talked about the regularity of it all, usually Friday nights or if Greg fell asleep, then Saturday morning before Camille woke up. Lately it was more like every other week, sometimes once a month, but it still happened.

Daniel was appalled by the sameness. Julienne just chalked it up to married life. Sex with Greg was like everything else. It was nice and consistent. She had craved a normal, safe life, and that is what she had. She and Greg knew what the other liked and neither wasted time and both were satisfied when it was over. No, she did not have exciting rooftop stories like Daniel, but she also knew exactly what she was getting.

Daniel shook his head some more. Julienne ignored him and turned up the radio. The temptations were singing and Julienne joined them:

I
Can turn the gray sky blue
I can make it rain, whenever I want it to, oh I
I can build a castle from a single grain of sand
I can make a ship sail, on dry land tell 'em yeah
But my life is incomplete and I'm so blue
'Cause I can't get next to you
I can't get next to you, babe (next to you)

When they got back to the cabin, Daniel stayed outside to smoke and sketch. Julienne went in with the idea she would read her book, but after two pages her eyes were drooping and she allowed herself a nap.

Julienne woke up not sure how long she had slept. She wandered into the kitchen and Daniel was putting the finishing touches on a mini nacho bar on the counter. Julienne didn't speak; she just grabbed a plate and let her stomach guide her: chips, lots of queso, some guacamole on the side, ground beef, and extra black olives.

Then she grabbed a napkin and headed to the sofa. She flipped through the channels until she landed on the CW's TV series of *Beauty and the Beast*. It wasn't quite the same as Disney's version, but it would do while she ate her nachos. Moments later, Daniel joined her. They ate in silence.

When she was done, she thought about getting up for seconds, but Daniel took her empty plate to the kitchen. Another episode of *Beauty and the Beast* began and Daniel returned with the fudge he'd bought earlier. Julienne took a piece and continued to watch this reimagining of her beloved Belle.

When the second episode was over, Julienne stretched and stood up.

"Thank you for dinner," she said to Daniel. "Those nachos were perfect."

"You're welcome," Daniel said, still sitting on the sofa. "Where are you going?"

"To clean," she said. Pointing at Daniel, "You cook." Pointing at herself, "I clean."

"Okay," Daniel said. "That's fair."

Julienne put up the leftovers, loaded the dishwasher, and then wiped the copper counters, which were original to the cabin. Daniel kept looking over his shoulder at her like he was waiting, but waiting on what she wasn't sure.

She opened the dishwasher to put in detergent and start it. When she stood up, Daniel was in the kitchen leaning on the counter.

"Okay, neighbor," Julienne acquiesced. "What's up?"

"You asked me a question last night," Daniel stated. The bruises on his face were faint. Time and the sun were helping the healing process.

"Okay," Julienne said, unsure of where Daniel was headed.

"You asked me what I wanted from you," Daniel continued.

"Yes," Julienne said. She was not sure she wanted to continue in this conversation. She might not like his request and the whole day had been just what she needed: no schedule, no demands, no shoulds.

Julienne had spent the whole day being in the present. She had not thought of the past nor had she worried about the future. She did not want whatever this conversation was to ruin it.

Daniel was on one side of the counter. She was on the other. He was so close yet the tone of this conversation made him feel a mile away.

Daniel leaned on his elbows and said, "I think you know what I want."

Julienne shook her head.

"I'm not following you." She turned away from him to grab a wineglass from the cabinet.

Daniel walked around and being taller, reached it much more easily from the second shelf. He handed it to her. She took it and then went to the fridge to pull out the bottle of wine. She poured the glass about halfway full and then let it sit. The wine was too cold and she decided to hold off before taking a sip.

Daniel watched her and waited until she met his eyes before he continued. Julienne leaned against the counter and folded her arms across her chest.

"You brought me here to get right."

Julienne nodded.

"But you also needed an escape."

Julienne started to protest, but he was right, so she nodded again.

"So maybe what I want is what you want."

Julienne stayed very still.

Daniel took the few steps to stand right in front of her.

"No matter what, Jules, we always lean on each other. Happy, sad, in between, we always turn to each other."

"Because we are best friends," Julienne said in her quiet voice.

"Are we?" Daniel asked, putting one hand on either side of her, pinning her to that section of the counter.

"Yes," Julienne nodded.

"Are you sure?" Daniel asked.

Julienne bit her lip.

"Dammit, Jules," Daniel said. "Don't do that."

"Do what?" Julienne asked.

"You know what," Daniel said, his voice low but firm. "And you know why."

Julienne ducked underneath his arm.

He was provoking her on purpose. She knew it. He knew it.

Julienne grabbed her glass of wine and headed to the deck. The sun was just beginning to set, making the sky look like it was on fire. The wind was blowing a little too hard, bringing with it the salty smell that only existed at the beach, and she wished she had something to pull her hair back with; instead, it was whipping around her face.

Julienne stood at the railing sipping her wine, letting the constant crash of the waves calm her down. Bringing him to the beach had seemed like a good idea, but at this moment she was not so sure. She did not want to fight with Daniel. He was so much a part of her, it was almost like fighting with herself.

Julienne heard the glass door slide open and then close, clicking back into place. She felt his footsteps. The wine bottle appeared in her periphery and without asking, he topped her glass off. Then he took a step back and sat in one of the deck chairs. They were Adirondack chairs left over from her parents. Years earlier Daniel had brought them new life by sanding them and painting them a glossy red. Julienne loved sitting in those chairs listening to the waves crash.

"You look so beautiful standing there like that," Daniel

said.

Keeping her back to him, she said, "Don't sweet-talk me right now."

"No, I'm serious," Daniel countered. "The sun is hitting your face just right. Your hair is swirling everywhere. Those big brown eyes looking out to the water. I could totally paint you like that."

Daniel always talked of painting her, but he never did. She sighed and took another sip of wine. Then she turned around to face him. He was the typical version of Daniel: no shirt, no shoes, and jeans low on his hips, with hair too long in his eyes.

"What do you want from me?" she pleaded.

"The truth," he said without hesitation.

She shook her head slowly from side to side. The days at the beach had darkened her olive skin. She had on shorts and one of Daniel's shirts, which was too big and hung off one of her shoulders. Her feet were bare and Daniel's pedicure skills with the red nail polish stood out. That was the closest he had ever come to painting her, she thought sarcastically.

"You know the truth," Julienne proclaimed.

Daniel stared at her like a sniper focused on a target.

Still holding her gaze, he said, "I want to hear you say it."

"Say what? You want to hear me say I love you. You know that. I've loved you since the first day I met you," Julienne admitted.

"Don't patronize me," Daniel said standing up. "You love ice cream, Jules. You love your dog. How do you really feel about me?"

Julienne took a big gulp of her wine.

"You know, I don't need to say it. That's our thing, isn't it," Julienne spat the words out. "We leave things unsaid."

"Not this time. Not here. Not now," Daniel said with force.

"God dammit," Julienne swore in a low voice.

Daniel took a step forward.

"Say it."

Julienne shook her head.

Daniel took another step forward.

"Say it."

Julienne crossed her arms, still holding on to her wineglass.

"You don't want to hear it."

"Yes, I do," Daniel insisted.

"You won't like it," Julienne retorted.

Daniel paused. A flicker went across his eyes. Julienne could almost see the cogs in his brain working. This was a possibility he had not considered. He looked away, taking in the waves just as she had done when she first walked out on the deck. Julienne drained the rest of her glass. Daniel turned his gaze back to her.

"Say it?" he asked this time.

"No," Julienne answered. She hated that in that moment she used her mom voice. She sounded no different than she did at the grocery store telling Camille no to cookies.

"Say it," he said, shouting this time.

"No," she shouted back.

He took another step towards her, and in a deliberate motion that surprised both of them, she threw her wineglass. The sound of the glass shattering mixed with the crashing of the waves. Julienne and Daniel both stood still.

Daniel, undeterred, put his hands on her shoulders. His hands were big, his touch warm, and any other time this would have been soothing. Broken bits of glass were everywhere.

"Say it," he whispered.

Julienne took a step back away from his touch.

She took a breath and looked back towards the water, which thanks to the Mississippi silt would never be a true blue. The Gulf Coast off of Galveston would always appear slightly muddy, like this situation. Nothing was clear; the waters were muddied.

"I think about it," Julienne conceded.

Daniel waited.

Julienne continued, still staring at the water.

"I think about what it would be like if you and I were together. You would be a painter, a local artist getting national attention. You would be featured in all the galleries downtown. The River Oaks crowd would be commissioning your work."

A small smile played on Julienne's lips as she delved into this other imagined world.

"And I, I would be a writer. Maybe I would have a column in the *Chronicle* or I'd be a regular contributor to *Texas Monthly*. Perhaps I would write that one great novel I know I have in me."

Julienne paused. Daniel waited, liking what he had heard so far.

"And we would live in one of those grand houses I love from the 1920s. Except ours would be a fixer-upper, which is why we got it for a song. We would do all the work ourselves, though, and make it ours."

Julienne was lost in her thoughts now.

"What about us?" Daniel asked.

Julienne looked at him now. Her hair was still swirling in the wind. Her cheeks rosy from the sun and her eyes so dark they were almost black against the blood orange sky.

"Us," she repeated. "Us in my imagination is unbelievable. You, in my mind, are unbelievable.

"Tell me," Daniel prodded. "Tell me how I am in your imagination."

Julienne closed her eyes.

"You, I, I think about how it would feel to have your hands on me every night. I think about how you would kiss me completely because you do everything completely. I think about you completely possessing me."

"When do you think about it?" Daniel continued.

"All the time," Julienne admitted.

"Where?" Daniel asked.

Julienne opened her eyes and looked at him. She was dressed but she felt naked. She took another deliberate breath and continued.

"In the shower," she answered.

"Really?" Daniel questioned.

She nodded yes.

"Where else?" he prodded.

"In my bed when Greg is out of town. I strip off all my clothes and get in those cold sheets naked. I think about where you would touch me, kiss me, and I come," Julienne admitted, even though she knew she should not be saying any of this out loud.

"You get off to me?" Daniel asked.

She nodded yes again.

"I make you wet," Daniel continued.

She nodded once more.

"Are you wet right now?"

Julienne kept nodding.

"How hard do you come?" Daniel inquired.

His voice was low and calm. He had moved to within inches of her. Her back was against the railing, which was holding her up. Julienne tipped her head back to look directly at him. His eyes were lit up; tonight, they appeared green. This was both good and bad for Julienne since green eyes were her favorite.

"The hardest," Julienne whispered.

Daniel put one hand at the base of her throat. Her breathing was shallow.

"Do you say my name?" Daniel asked.

"Yes," she said.

Daniel took the pad of his thumb and raked it across her bottom lip. Every nerve in Julienne's body tingled.

"Say it now," Daniel demanded.

He kept his hand at the base of her throat. Julienne looked at him with her big, dark eyes. She had been right. He knew all of this anyway, but a streak of cruelty that exists in every human being forced her to say it all out loud.

Biting her bottom lip, Julienne said his name in a whisper, "Daniel."

Daniel cocked his head to the left and bent down just a little to move in and kiss her, but Julienne stepped to the side. Her eyes narrowed.

"But however good you are in my fantasies, Daniel, in reality I know I would be a damned fool."

Daniel threw his arms out in exasperation.

"Jules, what are you talking about?"

Julienne took another step to the side to put more distance between herself and Daniel. She was beyond angry with herself and with him for having put all that out there. It should have stayed locked inside the recesses of her mind.

Raising her voice, she answered him, "In reality, I would be just another nameless girl you fucked at a bar. What's special about that?"

Julienne turned to go inside and in the last moment remembered the broken glass. She had meant to storm off, but instead she had to tiptoe among the remnants.

Any other time, Daniel would have laughed at her hopping through the glass, but not this time. His lips were set in a grim line as he watched her go back into the cabin.

Julienne was pacing inside the cabin like a dog in a cage. She wanted to go straight to bed or drink some more or throw something else. She didn't know what to do but she felt the need to do something. At this moment the cabin was too small. Daniel would eventually come back inside, and then what?

She opted for more alcohol and went to the kitchen for another bottle and a new glass. Julienne pulled out a bottle of Riesling even though she knew she was headed for a headache tomorrow. She concentrated on her movements. Using the corkscrew, she quickly opened the bottle. She poured herself a fresh glass and savored the first sip.

Julienne stood at the kitchen sink looking out the window. The view was the beach cabin next door. It was painted grey with white shutters. No one was there.

"Maybe I shouldn't be here," Julienne thought. At the time taking Daniel to the beach had seemed like the best idea, and standing her ground with Greg, staying at the beach had continued to be her choice. They were supposed to focus on Daniel, not her, not them.

The glass door opened and shut. Julienne stayed where she was. It felt like round two was about to ensue.

She heard his footsteps in the living room. At least he had left her alone in the kitchen. Julienne decided to face Daniel, which meant facing herself and all that she had just admitted out loud.

CHAPTER 12

In the end, she went to sleep by herself. He stayed on the sofa.

Daniel had wanted to talk more. Julienne had wanted to talk less. Daniel wanted to continue on in some fantasy where they were together as a couple. Julienne stayed rooted in their reality where she had an obligation to her husband, to her daughter.

In Julienne's mind the what ifs got them nowhere. In Daniel's mind, the what ifs were still possible.

Julienne wanted to put the cork back in the bottle. She wanted her best friend back and she wanted to continue on as they always had.

Daniel wanted something new.

At one point Julienne accused him of still reacting to Tara's news.

"Julienne, that's not fair," Daniel had pleaded.

"You still love her; you never got over her," Julienne retorted. "But you can't have her, and well, I'm just Jules. I have always been here in the sidekick role."

Julienne was pacing back and forth in front of the sofa

as she spouted her replacement theory.

Daniel put his hand on her shoulder to stop her movement. Julienne looked at his hand. In this moment, in this conversation, it was not good for him to touch her. She could feel Daniel staring at her, but Julienne refused to look up.

Daniel grabbed her chin and raised her face until their eyes met.

"Yes, I loved Tara and I married her and I envisioned our life to be quite similar to the one you have with Greg and Camille, but she and I didn't work," Daniel's breath was warm.

He kept his calloused hands on her chin and made sure she received every word he was saying. "One reason is I loved you first. She was never you, and it drives me crazy to see you settling on the life you have right now when we both could have so much more if we were together."

Julienne had no response but she continued to meet his gaze. Daniel looked like he wanted to kiss her again, but his attempt out on the deck had not gone so well. Another moment passed and Daniel let go.

Julienne just shook her head and turned her back to walk to the bedroom. Daniel watched her walk away and heard the words, "I can't." Then the bedroom door closed.

Julienne tossed and turned in the bed. She would kick one leg out and then get cold and pull up all the covers. She tried her side, her back, her stomach, but she could not get comfortable. Her physical movements matched the changing thoughts in her head. She should have taken advantage of having a whole bed to herself, but the bed felt too big, just like this situation with Daniel.

One moment she would tell herself her life was just

how it was meant to be. It was exactly what she had always wanted. Then she would change positions and let her mind indulge in the idea of being with Daniel, a whole Daniel, the man she knew he could be, not the man she picked up from jail.

Then she would think of her childhood and how he was her best friend and she did not want to change that dynamic. Regardless of leaving Greg behind, she did not want to ruin what they already had. If they tried and it did not work, there was no going back to just being friends.

With a sigh, she rolled over towards the nightstand to check the time on her phone. She touched the screen and the soft glow of Camille's face lit up the room. It was 1:06 a.m.

Julienne's mouth was dry and if she wanted to avoid that wine headache, she should take some aspirin and hydrate with some water. This meant getting out of bed and opening the door, which she had used to shut out her neighbor.

Julienne opened the door with caution, but the hinges were old and the door let out a long, low squeak. Julienne shook her head and continued out of the bedroom. She tiptoed through the living room. She saw Daniel's long form underneath a blanket on the sofa. His body was turned towards the cushions of the sofa, so Julienne could not see his face.

She made it to the kitchen where she got a bottle of water out of the refrigerator. She stood at the sink staring at the still empty beach house next door. She sipped on the water and made herself think of something else. A U2 song popped into her head, so she concentrated on those lyrics, reciting them in her mind:

I have climbed the highest mountains
I have run through the fields
Only to be with you
Only to be with you
I have run, I have crawled
I have scaled these city walls
These city walls
Only to be with you
But I still haven't found what I'm looking for

Julienne sighed because she would climb a mountain for Daniel, she would scale a wall for Camille, but she, herself, still had not found what she was looking for in life. Julienne found the aspirin in the cabinet and took two. She took another sip of water and put the half-full bottle back in the refrigerator.

Julienne reversed her tiptoe trek back to the bedroom. When she drew even with the sofa, Daniel had changed positions. He was now on his back. His left arm was behind his head and his right arm was flung out, hanging off the sofa.

The moonlight was streaming in through the sliding deck doors. Half of his face was lit up. His hair was flopping forward covering one eye. His cheekbones stuck out. His mouth was almost turned up and she wondered what was going on in his dream to almost cause a smile.

Out of habit, she pushed his hair back off his face. As always, his skin was warm. He turned his face toward her touch but stayed asleep. Looking at him in the moonlight like that, her neighbor, her Daniel, she gave up on thinking.

Julienne leaned down, pushed his hair back, and gave

his forehead a kiss. She waited for a reaction, but all Daniel did was sigh. Julienne leaned over again and placed a soft kiss on his lips. Daniel's eyes flew open. He started to say something but Julienne kissed him again, this time longer. She grabbed the blanket and slipped under it so they were both on the sofa.

On their sides facing each other, Daniel's face continued to be lit up by the moonlight. Julienne put her right hand on his cheek and kissed him again, slow and easy. His hand went to her hip. Her hand worked its way through his hair. His tongue darted in and out and left her wanting more of his kiss.

Daniel maneuvered himself on top of her with one hand behind her head and one at the small of her back. He looked into her eyes. The moonlight provided just enough illumination to see the look in his eyes. He was giving her an out in this pause, but she did not take it. She smiled and that was all he needed. He grabbed the back of her head and this time kissed her with urgency. She arched her back and melted into him. At that moment, she belonged to him.

Every kiss was long and deep and made her toes curl. Clothes came off but she could not tell you how. Daniel took his time and her body responded to every touch, every kiss. When he finally entered her, she exploded. She quivered for what seemed like forever and on an exhale, she said his name. He began to stroke her and she started all over. This time they came together. When they were done, he collapsed on top of her and he whispered in her ear: Jules.

With that, sleep came. She was warm and content tangled up in Daniel on the old worn-out sofa at her parent's beach cabin. Her worlds were colliding and there may be consequences, but in that moment, Julienne had found one thing she was looking for. Her neighbor had been there all along.

Julienne woke up the next morning in a tangle of blankets on the sofa. The moonlight had been replaced by the sunlight which was streaming in the living room and daring her to wake up. Julienne opened one eye and realized Daniel was not there. She stretched and tried to remain in the haze of sleep. Julienne was not ready to wake up, to think, to face the night before. She rolled over to her side facing the sliding glass doors and a swirl of smoke above the Adirondack chair caught her attention. Daniel was outside for his morning smoke.

Julienne stuck one foot out and smiled at her red toes. Then she stood up, wrapping the blanket around her. She took the three steps to the sliding glass doors and opened them. The wood was already warm from the morning sun. She noticed a pile of glass in the corner. Daniel had swept up her mess from the night before. This caused her second smile of the day.

Julienne stood in front of Daniel. He exhaled his most recent pull on the cigarette. Then he put it out in the ashtray. He pushed his hair out of his eyes and looked up to meet her gaze. His hair had streaks of light blond in it. His bruises were almost all gone. His chest was bare and tan. His eyes against the morning sun were green.

Julienne's initial urge was to crawl into his lap and have him for breakfast. Daniel cocked his head. Julienne bit her lip.

Daniel started to speak, but Julienne did not give him a chance. She leaned over to kiss him. He was a combination of sea salt, Old Spice, and menthol cigarettes.

"Jules," Daniel whispered as Julienne sat in his lap.

"Don't talk," Julienned requested. "Just kiss."

Daniel tugged on her blanket.

"What's going on under this?"

Julienned let go of the blanket as an answer.

Daniel's eyes grew big as he took in her naked form. Julienne's hair was a tangled mess from sleeping on the sofa. Her brown eyes refused to look away. She wanted Daniel and she didn't care in that moment. A breeze blew and Julienne's nipples responded. Daniel whistled. Julienned grinned.

Daniel cupped her right breast and just barely touched Julienne's nipple with his tongue. She sucked in her breath. Daniel teased her breasts again and again with the feathery touch of his tongue switching from one to the other. Julienne threw her head back and just reveled in the sun, the wind, and Daniel's mouth on her bare skin. Julienne began to grind against his erection and while Daniel continued to pay attention to her breasts, Julienne began to pleasure herself. When she came, she let out a cry of pure pleasure. In that moment Daniel entered her and she rode him with an intensity that surprised both of them. This time Daniel threw his head back and stared into Julienne's eyes as she rode him with a boldness even he did not even know she possessed.

When they were done, Julienne nestled her head in his shoulder. She focused on her breathing. Daniel's hands grazed her back and she could almost go back to sleep. Julienned let out a sigh. She could start every morning this way.

Daniel squeezed her behind.

Julienne raised her head in askance.

Daniel winked, "Well good morning, sunshine."

Julienne gave him a kiss on the neck and answered, "Good morning, neighbor."

Julienne stood up, wanting coffee and a shower. Daniel picked up the blanket which was crumpled on the side of the chair. He offered it to Julienne, who just shook her head. She walked back into the cabin naked. Daniel grinned and lit another cigarette.

After two puffs, he decided he wanted Julienne more than he wanted the nicotine. He followed her inside. The coffee maker was gurgling and he could hear the water running in the shower.

When he walked into the bedroom, Julienne was standing in front of the dresser staring into the mirror. One hand was on her chest. The other was pulling her hair back from her neck inspecting the whisker burns Daniel had left behind from last night and this morning. Julienne's white strips of skin stood in stark contrast to the rest of her tanned skin. Daniel decided they would need to get rid of all tan lines.

Daniel took a step forward and Julienne turned her head in his direction. She let go of her hair and crossed her arms in front of her chest.

"Don't," Daniel said

Julienne cocked her head. Daniel walked towards her and pulled her hands down.

"Don't do that," Daniel said. He came around behind her and put his arms around her waist. His chin rested on her head. He stared at her in the mirror. She looked at his reflection in the mirror.

"Don't look at me," he stated. "Look at yourself."

Julienne shook her head.

"Jules, look what we just did out on the deck for all the world to see," Daniel said. A creep of color started at the base of Julienne's throat and crept up into her face. Even through her tan, Daniel could see her blushing and this made him continue.

"Look in the mirror, Julienne," Daniel said in a low but firm voice.

Julienne closed her eyes.

Daniel whispered in her ear, "You are so sexy, Jules."

Julienne's eyelids opened in surprise.

"No, Daniel, we had hot sex, but me, I'm not sexy."

"Yes, Jules," he continued whispering in her ear. "You are."

Julienne gazed into the mirror. Their bodies standing there, his long and lean, hers with curves. They looked good standing together. She leaned into him a little and continued to stare and enjoy the warmth of him against her skin. He was right. She had completely given herself over last night and this morning, so why should she hold back now.

Daniel pulled her hair back and kissed the tattoo on the back of her neck.

"Tell me," Julienne said.

Daniel raised an eyebrow.

Julienne held his gaze in the mirror and continued, "Last night, you made me tell when I think of you, how I think of you. Your turn."

Daniel's lips turned up slightly but he had no answer.

"How often do you think of kissing me there," she indicated the back of her neck. "You said boys would have fun trying to kiss me there. Were you one of them? Tell me you think about it."

Daniel kissed her there again and it made her tingle.

"I have thought about it every day since you got that tattoo, Jules. I think about kissing you there every day."

Julienne smiled a Mona Lisa smile with her mouth closed, satisfied with the initial answer but still wanting to know more.

"What else," Julienne continued the questioning.

Daniel moved his hands to her breasts. He cupped them, and Julienne liked the feel of his hands on her. She liked standing there naked looking in the mirror with Daniel's hands on her body.

"I think about touching you," Daniel said quietly as his hands grazed the sides of her breasts and began making gentle circles, causing her to arch her back.

"I think about making you wet," Daniel kept going as one hand slipped down and began to stroke her.

"And now that I have heard you say my name, I will think about that every day, too," Daniel elaborated. Julienne had trouble standing still watching Daniel deftly tweak her right breast while his left hand continued to stroke her.

She started to turn around to face him. She wanted to be chest to chest, but he stopped her.

"Put your hand on the dresser," he ordered.

Julienne complied.

"Keep looking, Jules, and know how sexy you are."

Julienne braced herself as Daniel entered her. He put both hands on her hips and started slow.

Julienne stared in the mirror at him entering her and saw how good it felt on her face.

"Tell me," she ordered this time.

Daniel kept stroking her.

"Tell me how good it is," Julienne elaborated.

"It's so good."

"Tell me it's the best."

"You're the best."

Daniel turned up the intensity and Julienne met his rhythm and just as they were about to come together Julienne made one more request.

"Say it."

Julienne put one hand behind her to reach up and grab Daniel's neck just as Daniel's final thrust entered her.

"Julienne," Daniel said as he exhaled.

Julienne let go and leaned on the counter. Daniel collapsed on top of her. Julienne turned her head sideways to see their bodies still tangled in each other, spread out on the dresser this time instead of the sofa or the deck chair.

Daniel was breathing heavily. Julienne could stare at him naked all day, but together, well maybe they were sexy.

Julienne straightened up, which made Daniel stand up as well. The shower was still running and she could smell the French roast from the coffeemaker in the kitchen. Everything was normal and yet it was not.

Julienne took a step toward the shower and then looked over her shoulder at Daniel.

"Are we ever going to do it in the bed?" she asked with a smirk.

Daniel just chuckled but had no answer.

"Get in the shower, Jules."

"What are you going to do?" Julienne asked.

"Fix your coffee," Daniel answered.

Julienne grabbed his wrist.

"Fix me, instead," she requested. "In the shower," she expanded.

"Incorrigible," Daniel answered.

Julienned continued toward the shower with Daniel in tow.

"Are you complaining?" Julienne asked as she stepped into the shower.

"Absolutely not," Daniel answered with a wink as he joined her in the hot steamy stall.

After their shower, Julienne put on one of Daniel's T-shirts and some boy short briefs and then headed to the kitchen for her coffee. Her wet hair was wrapped up in a towel on her head. She savored the first sip. Daniel followed behind her with a towel wrapped around his waist. She waited for him to take his first sip and asked, "What do you want to do today?"

Daniel smiled a broad smile, something he did not do often.

"Jules, I have lots of ideas," He answered, "but two things are at the top of my list."

Julienne pulled one knee up against her chest and took another sip, waiting for him to go on.

"First, I want you to get rid of those tan lines," Daniel said matter-of-factly.

Julienne started to shake her head but stopped herself. She took another sip of coffee laden with creamer and said "Okay," like it was no big deal for straightlaced Julienne to lie out naked.

Daniel continued, "Second, I want to sketch."

Julienne nodded at this. Daniel had been sketching since they got to the beach. This one did not surprise her.

Daniel continued to look at her in question and then she realized her lying out naked and him sketching were connected.

Again, she started to protest but stopped. She nodded her head instead.

The morning had slipped by them with their deck, dresser, and shower activities.

They spent the afternoon on the deck. Julienne stayed lathered up in suntan lotion and read or slept. Daniel stayed busy sketching. She did not ask to see what he was sketching. He did not volunteer. Sometimes they talked; sometimes they did not. It was an easy afternoon.

Later, they cleaned up and went in search of food and music. On the one hand, it was no different than any other night with Daniel. They ate, they danced, and they laughed. It was all the same yet it wasn't. He held her the same way he always did when they danced and she rested her head on his shoulder and enjoyed the feel of his hand at the small of her back. Kenny Chesney sang:

And in the morning I'm leaving, making my way back to Cleveland
So tonight I hope that I will do just fine
And I don't see how you could ever be
Anything but mine

On Sunday they would return to Houston, but on that night in Daniel's arms she was still his, and so they danced.

Back at the cabin, Julienne washed her face and brushed her teeth. She put some lotion on and walked back to the bedroom. The room was dark with just a little moonlight coming in through the window. Daniel was already in bed lying on his back with his left arm out. Julienne crawled into bed and nestled into her neighbor.

She put her head on his shoulder and his arm went around her waist. Her left leg slid in between his and they were a perfect tangle. She sighed and closed her eyes, content in the warmth of him.

"I know you love me, Jules," Daniel said into the dark.

"I do," Jules confirmed.

A moment passed.

"And you know I love you," Daniel continued.

"Yes, Daniel, I know."

Another moment passed. Julienne broke the spell.

"But what we are doing here, it isn't real."

"Jules, this is many things, including real."

"No, Daniel, it's just us at the beach completely isolated. This does not translate back in Houston."

"It does if we want it to."

"So, what–I just move Greg out and move you in? I can't disrupt Camille's life," Julienne paused. "We aren't puzzle pieces we can just switch in and out."

Daniel interrupted. "I am not replacing Greg. I don't want your life, Jules. What you are doing right now–it isn't living. And what I'm doing–well, that isn't living either. You and I, we will live our lives with passion and authenticity. We will show Camille how to chase her dreams and we will make more babies and we will live a real life."

"I don't know, Daniel. You are always reacting to life. How do I know this, with me, here, isn't just another reaction?"

"Jules, you know it is not. And if it is, I have been reacting to you since that first day you pulled up into your aunt and uncle's driveway."

Julienne just held onto Daniel tighter.

Daniel kissed the top of her head. Then he kissed her forehead. She lifted her face and he kissed her on the lips. His hand went under her shirt; hers went in the waistband of his boxers. They moved slowly but not sweetly. Julienne loved Daniel but she also wanted to fuck him and this desire was new to her. Sex with Greg had become mundane, something to check off her chore list. Sex with Daniel was something else entirely.

Julienne moved on top of Daniel and took off her shirt. She set the rhythm and enjoyed being in control. At one point, Julienne leaned over and whispered in Daniel's ear, "You can fuck all the short blond women you want, but they will never be me."

Daniel's eyes grew big as he gripped her hips tighter.

"You're right, Jules, they will never be you."

Later when they were collapsed on each other, Daniel kissed her shoulder and followed with, "Jules, I love the way you fuck me."

Julienne just smiled and went to sleep with not one thing figured out, but happy anyway.

When she woke up the next morning, Julienne still had no idea what she was going to do. Their week at the beach was up. Julienne wished they had come in separate cars. She wished she could just creep out of bed, grab her stuff, and leave. That wouldn't solve anything, but it would make her exit easier. She could just leave her neighbor sleeping and pretend this week hadn't happened–except it had.

On that Sunday morning, they drank their coffee in silence. Julienne figured Daniel was probably wishing for his own car right about now as well. After coffee, they packed up their things and put the cabin back together until the next time someone came to visit. Julienne missed Camille and her life in Houston was waiting on her. She had no idea if this week had helped Daniel at all or if it had just served to make his life even more twisted. She could only focus on Daniel because she could not even begin to consider how the week had affected her, not yet anyway.

On the way out of town, she stopped one last time at St. Mary's Church. Daniel stayed in the car, but Julienne went inside to light a candle. On most visits she prayed for her parents, but today she prayed for Daniel and for herself. As she was making the sign of the cross to end her prayer, a woman came out of the confessional looking flushed. Maybe she was embarrassed by the sins she had just confessed, or maybe she... Julienne just shook her head at her own fantasy and smiled.

The drive back took less than an hour. As they got closer to Houston, the knot in Julienne's stomach grew. The downtown skyline had always meant home, but today it meant something else. Daniel just continued to stare out the passenger window.

When they pulled up into his driveway, Julienne put the car in park, turned down the radio, and turned to look at Daniel. His face was almost healed all the way, and the sun and sleep had helped. He looked good. He looked like her neighbor.

He grabbed her hand and kissed it.

"Come inside," he asked.

She shook her head no. If she went inside, she knew what would happen and she was just prolonging going home.

"Now what?" Daniel asked.

"Let's take some time," Julienne suggested.

Daniel continued to hold her hand.

"What does that mean?"

Julienne took a breath and elaborated, "Let me have the rest of the summer. Let me focus on Camille and more importantly focus on myself. Let me figure out what I really want."

"Okay," Daniel said with not much confidence.

"And you can use this time, too," Julienned added.

"How so?"

"Daniel, a week ago I was picking you up from jail. You can use some time to focus on yourself. What do you really want? And do you really want me, or am I just another Band-Aid?"

Daniel started to protest, but Julienne continued.

"We love each other and nothing changes that. Nothing changes what we have been to each other since we were kids. Maybe we were just being there for each other this week or maybe we discovered something even more about us, but either way, we need time. I need time, Daniel," Julienne pleaded.

Daniel's face tensed, showing the lines around his eyes, and she could see he wanted to argue. She put her hands on either side of his face.

"I will always be yours," Julienne said with tears in her eyes.

Daniel kissed her forehead.

"Nothing will change my mind, Jules," he declared. "But you are right; I could use some time to continue to get myself right, to be the man who can give you the life you really deserve."

In the end, she made him promise radio silence until Labor Day. Then they would meet at the beach and see where they stood. They continued to sit in her car in his driveway holding hands.

Julienne looked up at him, and he was, well, he was everything and she had no idea if this was a good plan. Everything was jumbled and this was the only fair way she could see to find a way out.

Daniel squeezed her hand and leaned in to kiss her. This kiss was long; he lingered and she let him. His warm hands were on either side of her face. She clutched the front of his shirt. She did not want the kiss to end but it did. Daniel gave her one more forehead kiss and then he was out of the car and in his house, seemingly in all one motion.

Julienne continued to sit. She wanted to go in after him. Instead, she put the car in reverse and backed out of the driveway. As she drove away from Daniel's house, she turned the radio back up. U2 was singing:

You say you want
Diamonds on a ring of gold
You say you want
Your story to remain untold
But all the promises we make
From the cradle to the grave
When all I want is you

All Julienne could do was drive and cry.

CHAPTER 13

Julienne would never forget the day she got the news. It was a Thursday afternoon in August 2008. The sun was shining, but there was a hint of breeze. Julienne had on a sleeveless top with spaghetti straps, and while the sun felt good on her shoulders, every time the wind blew, she wanted to go back inside and grab a sweater. It had been a little over a month since the trip to the beach. School was just around the corner.

Julienne was sitting on the back porch watching six-year-old Camille play in her house her godfather had built her. He had kept his promise after her birthday party when she turned four. He had come over three weekends in a row to put the playhouse together. He never came in the house. He never spoke to Julienne. He did make his goddaughter happy.

Gaston, their rescue pup, was back and forth between the yard and the playhouse, which Camille also claimed was a doghouse for him as well. The miniature house was yellow with white shutters. It looked exactly like the house Julienne had described wanting to live in when she was twelve. She knew it; Daniel knew it. He had built the playhouse for her daughter, but it was a gift to her as well.

Julienne remembered exhaling and letting out a long breath. She needed to do some laundry and probably get supper started, but sitting in the sun watching her daughter was a stolen moment of peace and she wanted it to last longer. She wanted to continue to sit in the calm nothingness of this moment before she had to deal with life and all of its messiness.

Things had been tense with Greg ever since she had returned from the beach. He would not let go of the fact that she went, nor would he try to understand why she went. He just remained mad.

Julienne remained confused. Yesterday, she had taken Camille to Three Brothers Bakery for the first time for cinnamon rolls and hot chocolate. She had told Camille how this was her favorite bakery, but what she meant was that it was her favorite bakery with Daniel. Her uncle brought them there when they were kids to let them pick out a treat, and later when they could drive, it was the best way to bribe the other to do what they wanted. Neither ever said no to a bag with the Three Brothers' logo on it. It was Julienne's idea to have no contact, but being at the bakery that was one of their places somehow was comforting to her. Then Julienne looked down at her daughter, who wanted to know if they could bring a cinnamon roll home for Daddy, and Julienne was right back to confused.

Last week, while she was out running errands, she passed the Astrodome, once touted as the eighth wonder of the world. On the one hand it reminded her of her childhood, baseball games cheering on the Astros. She liked Jose Cruz; Daniel's favorite player was Nolan Ryan. Daniel's dad would get them tickets to a Sunday afternoon game, and they would both wear their matching Astros baseball hats. Julienne didn't like the crowds and always held Daniel's hand in the corridor, but once in their seats, she cheered the loudest. She and Daniel would always share a dome dog and to this day that was still the best hot dog she'd ever had. And now the Astrodome just sat there in all of its dilapidated glory, dwarfed by its successor. The city did not know what to do with the Astrodome. On the one hand, the building was a sentimental favorite; on the other hand, it was just a falling-down building that served no purpose now. The city's indecision on the dome matched her own where Daniel was concerned.

It was this indecision that kept her glued to her chair watching her daughter and their dog play outside.

Last night at dinner Julienne had asked Greg if he was ever going to let it go. He did not answer her. He had gone straight to bed. Julienne had kept busy in the kitchen cleaning and then reorganizing the pantry. Meanwhile, the same radio tucked in the corner kept her company:

I'm good at seein' the signs
I'm good at reading between the lines
No use in hangin' on
'Cause you're good to go
And, baby, I'm good as gone

Julienne wondered if she was good as gone. She had no answer and ended up falling asleep on the sofa watching *Beauty and the Beast* reruns on the CW. Now here she was enjoying her afternoon with her daughter and her dog and procrastinating on living her life. She could not imagine tonight's dinner would go much better; hence the procrastination.

Then this morning Greg had surprised her, striding into their bedroom after she thought he had left for work. Julienne, wrapped in a towel fresh from her shower, was standing in front of the mirror. While she was looking at herself, she was also remembering standing in front of a mirror at the beach with Daniel behind her. Her tan was still present, her hair dripping wet, and she was wishing she could crawl back into bed, but only if the right person was there to crawl into bed with.

Greg mumbled something about forgetting a paper for work and Julienne stayed rooted to her spot in front of the mirror. Then Greg stopped and looked at her. It was the first time he had truly looked at her since she returned from the beach. There stood her husband in his usual grey and blue with his light brown hair brushed back from his face. His light brown eyes went up and down her body.

Julienne waited.

"Nice tan," Greg said and then walked out.

Julienne blushed. Then she got dressed and blow-dried her hair and went to check on Camille.

The dog barking brought her out of her reverie that afternoon. She stood to check on Gaston and Camille, but then her phone was ringing. She looked down to see David's name on the screen. Before she could answer the phone, someone was knocking on her door. Julienne looked out to see her uncle's truck in her driveway. Then her phone pinged indicating a text, and Greg's picture popped up. Gaston was still barking and Camille was calling out to her, "Watch me, Mommy. Watch me."

Julienne made eye contact with her daughter and smiled.

She was making her way to the front door and trying to call back David at the same time. She was not expecting her aunt and uncle and David almost never called her. Daniel's brother sent funny texts, but he never called. As she opened the door, David answered the phone. Her uncle blurted out his news, but then again so did David over the phone. They were saying the same thing, but she could not process it. Her front door was open. Her hand held her cell phone to her ear. Her uncle said it again. David said it again. Maybe they both said it in unison.

Julienne remembered it felt like she got sucker-punched in the gut. She walked away from the front door and dropped the cell phone. She had to grip the back of the grey tufted sofa to remain upright and not let the pain take her down. Daniel had pointed out her penchant for tufting. She liked tufting on a sofa, on a purse, even on a shoe. She never noticed she was a sucker for tufting till Daniel made light of it. She wanted to smile at the thought of this while she held on tight, but no one would understand why.

Other words floated around her: car wreck, swerved for a dog, ambulance, pronounced dead on the scene.

Julienne did not respond to any of the words floating around her head. She just kept shaking her head in affirmation even though she did not really understand what her uncle and David were trying to tell her.

People just seemed to appear out of nowhere. At one point Julienne noticed Daniel's dad was sitting on her sofa with his head in his hands. Her aunt and uncle were keeping busy in the kitchen but doing what she wasn't sure. Several pings later, Greg had rushed into the house and just kept hugging everyone. Greg was not exactly a hugger so she found his affection off-putting but no one else seemed to notice. Her phone was still on the floor in the foyer. She had not read any of Greg's texts.

Daniel's brother, David, had shown up with his girlfriend. Julienne could not remember her name. They took turns crying as well while sitting on her grey tufted sofa.

Julienne stayed rooted to the same spot holding on to the sofa. With all the commotion going on she realized Camille was still outside. She turned to get a glimpse of her daughter. Camille was coming out of her yellow playhouse with white shutters that Daniel had made for her. Camille waved at her mother. She waved back.

Julienne could not move from that spot. She could not speak. She still could not register what they were saying. She refused to process it. The only thing she could do was wave at her daughter.

Eventually, everyone left with plans to meet in the morning. Greg took Camille upstairs to start her bath. Julienne looked down at her hands. Her knuckles were white from gripping the sofa for so long. She could no longer feel her fingers and when she let go the pain from the blood pumping back through hurt in the best possible way. This was a pain she could deal with.

Julienne went to the kitchen and got a bottle of water from the fridge. Then she retrieved her phone from the foyer. The home screen showed missed calls, voicemails, and texts. None of which she cared about.

She went out to the backyard. This was the last place, the last moment where she felt peace, where everything was still possible. She looked up at a half-moon and a handful of stars. She took a ragged breath. She felt everything and nothing all at the same time.

Julienne entered her security code on her phone. She listened to the first voicemail; she heard the same message again: Daniel is dead.

She threw the phone and it landed with a thud against the side of the yellow playhouse. She half laughed, half cried and the sound was strange to her. Julienne had not been able to make a decision and so the universe had made it for her.

Her neighbor, her Daniel, was dead.

Julienne sunk to the ground and wrapped her arms around her knees and rocked back and forth. She should cry, she should scream, she should do a lot of things, but she just made herself breathe and look at the stars and repeated to herself over and over again, Daniel is dead.

The next day Julienne spent helping Daniel's dad with funeral arrangements. Yellow roses were a yes. Sappy songs were a no. Mr. Hawk asked Julienne to give the eulogy. Greg did not think it was a good idea, but Julienne had never said no to Daniel, and in this instance, she would not say no to his dad, either.

When Julienne got home, her aunt and uncle kept trying to feed her, but she wasn't hungry. Greg poured her a glass of red wine. She drank instead. Her aunt and uncle put up all the food and went home. Greg put Camille to bed. Julienne finished the bottle of wine.

After Greg went to bed, Julienne grabbed her keys and drove to Daniel's house. She wandered through the rooms. He still had the leather couch they had found at the estate sale. The front bedroom had become his painting space but Julienne did not want that room.

She went to the back to his bedroom. The bed was unmade. Next to the bed was a Nicholas Sparks book and a picture of them from their New Orleans trip. His arm was around her shoulders. The "J" necklace he had just given her around her neck. They were both smiling. The bartender had taken the picture for them. She did not realize he still had it. She figured he must've put the picture in the drawer when girls came over, and that thought almost made her smile. She picked up the picture and touched his face. His smile in that picture was almost too much to bear so she put the picture down.

She turned to his dresser and opened the top drawer on the left where he kept his T-shirts. She stripped off her clothes and put on one of his worn T-shirts. Julienne climbed into his bed. She held on to his pillow and told herself to breathe.

Daniel's bed, Daniel's shirt, it all smelled like him. Julienne tried to pretend he was there with her; his head at the other end just like when they were kids. His smell was a comforting mix of Camel Blues cigarettes and Dolce & Gabbana light blue cologne. He had been smoking that brand since high school; she had always bought him that scent. But all of this was a poor substitute for her neighbor. She could not close her eyes.

Instead, she continued to breathe in his scent and stare up at the ceiling. Part of her wasn't completely surprised to get this news. In the wake of his divorce from Tara, she had mentally prepared herself for it. He was drinking too much and sleeping around too much and she had figured that behavior would catch up to him and it almost had.

On a random Thursday night, while she was sitting at the dining room table grading essays, there had been a knock on her door. Looking out the window, she saw a yellow taxicab. Opening the door, she peeked her head out to see Daniel. He was leaning against the arched portico; his eyes were closed.

"Daniel," she said his name.

He opened his eyes slowly.

"Jules," he said the familiar nickname. "Can you pay the man?"

"Seriously?" Julienne had asked.

Daniel had just nodded his head and then closed his eyes.

Julienne grabbed her wallet from her purse sitting on the bench in the entryway and went outside to pay the taxi.

"Hi," Julienne said to the cab driver through the window. His response was to hold out his hand. She handed him the credit card; he handed it back to her when the transaction was processed and drove away.

Julienne just shook her head as she walked back up to her front door. Daniel was still leaning against the archway. The porch light both highlighted and shadowed him all at the same time. Julienne came around to stand in front of Daniel and touched his shoulder.

Daniel opened his eyes.

"Jules," he said. "This was the only place I could think of to come."

"Okay, Daniel," Julienne answered. He had on a white button-down shirt, jeans, and a navy blazer. His hair was rumpled but other than that, he looked fine. But dropped off by a cab posted up on her front porch on a Thursday night was not fine.

"Are we staying on the porch or are you coming inside?" Julienne asked.

"I think," Daniel hesitated. "I think I need a Band-Aid"

Julienne started to ask why but Daniel moved his blazer aside to reveal a rip in his shirt outlined by red. Julienned stepped forward and pulled his shirt up. Daniel had about a three-inch slice on the left side of his stomach that was oozing blood.

Julienne inhaled.

Daniel pulled his shirt down.

"Daniel, what–" Julienne started to ask but Daniel just stood up straight and reached out for the handle of the front door.

"You need to see a doctor," Julienned stated. Daniel opened the front door. Julienne followed but continued, "You might need stitches."

Daniel walked through the dining room to the kitchen and sat down at the breakfast table.

"Jules," Daniel winced. "I don't have insurance. You're a great mom which means I know you have a first aid kit: peroxide, antibiotic ointment, Band-Aids, please."

Julienne just stared at Daniel sitting in her kitchen. He stared back. They both heard footsteps but neither looked away.

"Julienne," Greg questioned as he walked through the living room towards the kitchen. "Is everything–" he stopped when he saw Daniel. Greg just shook his head and kept walking through the kitchen out to the garage.

Julienne shook her head as well and went to retrieve the first aid kit from their bathroom. When she returned Greg was sitting with Daniel, and they were both drinking a beer.

"So, you didn't know she was married?" Greg asked.

"Nope," Daniel responded.

"And you only got together the one time?" Greg asked.

"Yep," Daniel confirmed.

"And the husband found you and made his point, so to speak," Greg continued.

Daniel laughed and then winced, "Yep."

"Huh," Greg said. Then they both took a swig of beer.

Julienne opened up the first aid kit. Daniel pulled up his shirt. Greg gave Daniel a slap on the shoulder and left the room. Julienne did the best she could with the wound, which wasn't as deep as it was wide.

Daniel slept on the sofa. Julienne called his brother, David, to let him know what happened and to guarantee Daniel a ride in the morning. Then Julienne proceeded to get up every two hours to check on Daniel, much like she had done when Camille was a baby. The next day, Daniel went home with his brother and life continued on in the Eversole household.

She had expected a scene from Greg, but the next morning while he was shaving and she was applying makeup he made the comment, "That's rough. I mean, he didn't know she was married."

He shook his head and then rinsed his razor. Julienne took a sip of coffee. She waited. Greg said nothing else. They both continued to get ready for work.

Julienne breathed in Daniel's scent again as she pulled the covers up tighter in his bed. She rolled over on her side and held his pillow tight.

The morning of the funeral, Julienne stood in front of the closet. She could not decide what to wear. She couldn't decide what to tell Camille, either. She had tried earlier to explain to Camille that her godfather was in heaven. Camille had nodded her head and then asked to watch

Beauty and the Beast. Greg had just shrugged his shoulders. Now Camille was going on a playdate while she and Greg went to the funeral, Daniel's funeral.

Julienne continued to stare into her closet. Two hands squeezed her shoulders and Greg said, "Julienne..."

He didn't finish and she just grabbed his hand and they stood there together.

"Look at the time," Greg commented, letting go, and Julienne took the hint.

At the funeral Julienne cleared her throat and secretly wished she had something to drink, like a shot of whiskey. Instead, she touched the pearls around her neck as if that somehow would help. The church was full and a bunch of eyes stared up at her, waiting. From the podium, she glanced to her left. There laid a dark mahogany coffin that housed her neighbor. On a table sat a vase of yellow roses and a picture of Daniel smiling, showing off the playhouse he had completed for Camille.

Julienne turned her head back to the congregation. In the front row were Daniel's dad and his brother. They both looked worn down, but Daniel's dad attempted to smile at her. She wanted to comfort him. In his face she saw what Daniel would have looked like as an older man. Mr. Hawk still had a full head of hair, but it was shot through with grey, almost making his dark blond hair look like it was highlighted. Daniel inherited his grin from his father, and she imagined the same creases in his dad's face would have shown up in his.

In the third row sat Tara. Her hair was still frosted and teased into a flipped-up bob. She wore the same pink lipstick and too much mascara. She looked almost the same except for a few more lines around her eyes. She was sniffing but not actually crying. Julienne did not want her here. Tara had only caused Daniel pain in life, and she had no right to sit here and accept sympathy because her ex-husband was dead. Tara kept her eyes down staring at nothing. She had not yet made eye contact, but Julienne felt the need to make her uncomfortable so she stared a moment longer.

The priest cleared his throat from his seat in the pulpit. Julienne realized she had been standing too long and probably needed to stay something. She glanced at her notes, took a breath, and began:

"I met Daniel when I was eight years old. It was in the afternoon in the fall and George Strait was playing on the car radio. We had just buried my parents, and I was going to live with my aunt and uncle. Daniel lived next door. Back then he was super skinny–all eyes, teeth, and kneecaps. He took one look at me, this quiet girl in a black dress, and for some inexplicable reason he offered to be my friend.

I do not know if it is ironic or if Daniel and I have just come full circle, but our friendship began on the day of a funeral. And now..."

Julienne paused. She could feel the tears at the back of her eyes. She swallowed hard and willed herself to continue.

"And now, here we are at a funeral except this time with an end instead of a beginning.

Back then starting with that first funeral, I never spoke. Daniel did all my talking for me, so I know he is taking pleasure in the fact that I am speaking on his behalf today."

This elicited a few chuckles from the audience.

Julienne gave a half-smile and looked out at Greg, who gave her a wink. She knew it was wrong to rely on Greg in this moment. She had no right to take comfort from this man in order to bury another, but she did.

Julienne took another breath and continued:

"From the very beginning, ours was an odd friendship that somehow always worked. When I was happy or sad or anything in between, I always had my neighbor to lean on no matter what. And I tried to be there for him in return.

Even though on paper, Daniel and I were complete opposites, we found common ground. We both liked musicals. His favorite was *Guys and Dolls* and I am probably in trouble for sharing that with you. We are both suckers for a Nicholas Sparks novel. We got our tattoos together. We both love the beach. It's where he did his best painting and according to him, my best writing. We both adore Van Morrison and it's a rule that no matter where we are when 'Brown Eyed Girl' comes on, we dance.

Over the years people tried to pin down our relationship.

Were we like brother and sister? Yes, I guess, in that I considered him my family.

Were we best friends? Yes, in that he was the longest and most loyal friend I ever had.

Did we love each other? Of course, I loved him with all my heart.

In my mind, I always simply thought of him as my neighbor.

For me, the word neighbor encompassed all those things: family, friendship, love, and so much more, like loyalty and trust.

I know from the outside looking in, Daniel probably appeared to be this free spirit who lived in the moment and was never really pinned down.

And while that is true, for me he was a safe harbor; for me he has always been an anchor in my life."

Julienne paused to take in the room. Tara continued to look at her shoes. Daniel's dad and brother were nodding their head in affirmation of her words. Greg was still watching her, trying to encourage her even though he had not wanted her to speak. She glanced again at the coffin. There was never any doubt she would speak for her neighbor. Another breath. She shifted her weight from side to side in the black high heels. She had felt the need to be tall today like somehow the extra height would help.

"I am not sure what life will be like without Daniel. Who will call me Jules? Who will bring me a blizzard from Dairy Queen on a random Tuesday night and then wake me up the next morning to go run it off?

I have no idea where I would be in life without Daniel. I might have stayed silent as a child. I definitely would not have gotten this tattoo. I don't know that I would have had the courage to have Camille. I would not have believed it possible to have the life I have now, if Daniel would not have told me it was possible and more importantly that I was worthy of it.

You are all here today to celebrate his life, so remember him at his best, forgive his imperfections, and honor him by living in the present and taking nothing for granted.

For me, I know I will forever be shaped by his presence in my life. I will never forget him, and I will always love my neighbor, Daniel."

Julienne locked eyes with Daniel's dad. He nodded his head in approval and tried his best to give her a grin. The gesture damn near broke her because it was the closest thing she had to Daniel. She gripped the podium and held his gaze. Then the organist began to play. Julienne gathered her notes and took her spot on the front row with the family. Julienne was not sure she should be sitting there; she wasn't sure she deserved the honor, but Daniel's dad had insisted.

She could not tell you what the rest of the ceremony was like. She just sat there and willed herself to get through it.

Later at the cemetery, people lingered. Julienne remembered lots of hugging. Greg told her she did a good job. Her aunt said she was proud of her. Daniel's dad seemed to want her near so she stayed by his side.

Julienne had not noticed Tara at the cemetery, but in a moment there she was with her pink frosted lipstick and flipped-up bob standing in front of her and Daniel's dad.

Julienne put her hand on Mr. Hawk's back and stared at Tara just like she had done at the church. No one spoke.

Daniel's dad shifted his weight and said, "Well, thank you for coming today. I appreciate it."

Tara nodded her head. She took a step as if to walk away but then she stopped and said, "I hope you know I did love him."

Daniel's dad started to answer, but under her breath Julienne said, "No, you didn't."

"Excuse me," Tara said, at last making eye contact with Julienne.

With more conviction, Julienne said, "No, you didn't."

Tara shook her head, "I'm not going to argue with you,

Julienne."

"Good," Julienne smirked, "It's probably best you go."

Tara held her stare. Daniel's dad shifted his weight again.

"I am leaving, but don't kid yourself, Jules," she said, almost spitting out the nickname. "You were no better for him than I was."

Julienne wanted to ask her what she meant, but this time Tara did take a step away and then another until she was at her car and driving away.

Julienne still had her hand on Mr. Hawk's back and he swung his left arm around her shoulders.

"Come on, Julienne," he said. "Let's go."

As they walked back to the car the funeral home had provided them, Mr. Hawk squeezed Julienne's shoulder and said, "She's just upset, Julienne. You were always good for my son."

Julienne just nodded. If Daniel had lived, that statement may not have held true. She might have broken his heart just like Tara. However, Daniel was gone and she had tried. Julienne had tried to be good to Daniel like he had been good to her.

When Julienne got home that night, she had the house to herself. Her aunt and uncle had Camille. Greg had gone back up to the office to finish work he had missed from the funeral.

Walking up the front walk, Julienne was considering what she wanted. Julienne wanted out of her black dress. She wanted a glass of wine, maybe a cigarette. She had taken a pack from Daniel's house. She wasn't sure why. She always wanted him to quit.

Julienne's list was interrupted by a large rectangle

package on her front porch. It was addressed to her, but she had not ordered anything. There was no return address.

Julienne opened the front door and lugged the package inside. She went in the bedroom to change. She washed her face free of makeup and put Daniel's shirt back on with her favorite grey sweats. She turned on the radio in the kitchen and retrieved some scissors to help her open the package. Kenny Chesney sang:

I'm built to fade like your favorite song
I get reckless when there's no need
Laugh as your stories ramble on
Break my heart but it won't bleed
My only friends are pirates, it's just who I am
I'm better as a memory than as your man

Memories were all she had now of Daniel. She came back to the foyer with the scissors to open the package.

She pierced the center seam and opened the cardboard box. Inside was a canvas wrapped in a bunch of bubble wrap. She used the scissors again to get through the protective covering. She pulled from the top down and saw a sun setting in the night sky.

She pulled the canvas up out of the wrapping and set it face-up on the dining room table.

Julienne stepped back and her hand went to her mouth. The painting was her. She was standing on the deck at the cabin with the fiery orange sky, the waves, and the shore behind her. The brushstrokes were wide and the colors were vibrant.

Her dark hair was swirling around her shoulders. She

was in a cream sundress standing on her toes looking out at the view. Her face showed the blush from the sun and he made her eyes even bigger and darker than they were in real life.

Julienne knew she was not that striking or exotic, but in Daniel's eyes, in his painting she was. She checked the package for a note, but there was none. Just the painting with Daniel's signature in the corner.

Her neighbor had painted her.

Julienne continued to stare at the painting. Then her stomach twisted and she barely made it to the bathroom before she threw up.

CHAPTER 14

March 2019

When they got home from the hospital, the house was empty. Julienne sent Hawk upstairs to his room. Gaston headed for the backyard. Julienne texted Camille, who texted back her plan to go over to her friend's house after school to work on a project unless her mom needed her.

Julienne told her to please work on her project and dinner would be waiting when she got home. Julienne continued to unload the car and unpack everything they had accumulated at the hospital. Every time she passed the painting, the evidence of her week at the beach, she wanted to feel bad, but she did not.

She called her aunt and uncle to let them know she was home. They confirmed they would be over tomorrow to sit with Hawk so Julienne could return to work. She started a load of clothes in the washing machine, checked on Hawk, who was playing video games in bed, and then went to sit outside. After all those days in the hospital, it was good to just be outside and breathe.

The playhouse still stood in the corner of the yard. Flashes of Camille and Hawk playing in it when they were younger made her smile. The yellow playhouse made by Daniel always made her smile. Like the painting, the miniature house told her all she needed to know.

Although it could not answer any questions about Greg. Julienne picked up her phone, scrolled through her contacts, and called Greg.

She pulled her feet up underneath her and waited while the phone rang. After four rings, it went to voicemail. Julienne hung up. She texted instead, one word: home.

Julienne took another breath and went back inside. Gaston followed her.

She checked on Hawk again, who was still playing video games. He nodded yes when she suggested pizza.

Julienne placed the order and continued to keep busy wandering from room to room, starting in the kitchen where she unloaded the dishwasher. Then she wandered into the living room and folded the blanket on the sofa and put it back in the basket next to the sofa.

She was curious why it was out. Julienne was the only one who ever used it. Greg would tease Julienne about always being cold. Julienne was the one who wrapped up with the blanket when watching TV. She would just smile at Greg and snuggle into the blanket with Gaston usually snuggled up beside her.

Julienne stared at the sofa and then went back to their bedroom. The bed was made and each toss pillow was in the right spot.

Greg never made the bed. Julienne thought back to the blanket on the sofa. She wondered if Greg had been sleeping there. Julienne shook her head at the thought.

The afternoon became the evening moving along at a

quiet pace. Pizza was eaten, laundry was folded, lunches were made for the next day. Camille made it home. Hawk went to bed. Julienne decided what to wear to work–pencil skirt and button-down shirt.

Julienne felt like she was treading water. Greg would determine which way the tide would go from here. At 9:30 Julienne gave up on creating stuff to do and crawled into bed. She grabbed her copy of *Wuthering Heights*. She was rereading the novel in an act of solidarity with her students.

In the book, Catherine stated: "He's more myself than I am. Whatever our souls are made of, his and mine are the same."

As Julienne read this, all she could think of was Daniel. The only problem was Daniel was dead. Greg was alive. Julienne gave up on reading. She put the book on her nightstand, turned off the lamp, and rolled over on her side to go to bed.

The next day after work Julienne parked in front of the familiar house. When she had moved in with her aunt and uncle, she had–with one invitation to play from Daniel–basically moved into the Hawk household as well. As a child, wherever Daniel was, that was where Julienne wanted to be.

Julienne turned off the ignition but did not get out of the car right away. Mr. Hawk had always been patient with his son's dark-haired friend who never spoke. She remembered the way he kept her close at the funeral. She saw Daniel in him and she guessed he saw his son's friend.

She knew Greg would never forgive her. She knew Mr. Hawk might not either once she told him. She was not sure which was worse.

Her aunt and uncle no longer lived next door. Walking up the path to the front door as an adult was different from entering through Daniel's bedroom window as a child.

Julienne stood in front of the door and took a breath. If she were one of her students, she would call herself out for procrastinating. She shook her head and then lifted her hand to press the doorbell, when the door opened.

"Who died?" asked Mr. Hawk with one hand on the door as if for support.

"No one," Julienne shook her head.

"I saw you pull up," Mr. Hawk nodded toward her car. "You are taking your time. You aren't smiling," Mr. Hawk shrugged. "Looks like bad news to me."

"No one died," Julienne reiterated. "I mean, besides Daniel."

Mr. Hawk's shoulders slumped and he opened the door wider for Julienne to come in.

"Sweetheart, that was a long time ago."

"I know," Julienne admitted, stepping over the threshold. "It just doesn't feel like it."

Mr. Hawk didn't respond. He just gave her shoulder a squeeze as they walked into the kitchen.

He offered her something to drink, but she shook her head and took a seat at the kitchen table. It was the same table with an oak top and whitewashed legs that she had sat at as a kid.

Mr. Hawk sat across from her. His first name was Donald, but that never felt right, so she stuck with Mr. Hawk.

"Well," he prompted.

"It's, it's about Hawk," Julienne stuttered.

Mr. Hawk sat up a little straighter. "I thought he was

doing better."

"He was, he is," Julienne affirmed.

"Okay," Mr. Hawk waited.

"Well, it's just, I need..." Julienne stumbled. "I don't know how to say this."

Mr. Hawk arched his thick, snow-white eyebrows.

Julienne squared her shoulders, looked Mr. Hawk in the eyes, and said, "Hawk is Daniel's son."

Mr. Hawk returned the eye contact and his mouth maintained a grim line. Julienne waited for more of a reaction. They both continued to stare.

Seconds passed and Mr. Hawk leaned back into the wooden chair and said, "I know."

Julienne's eyes widened.

"Well, I didn't know at first," Mr. Hawk offered. "But, my goodness, he looks just like Daniel, and then when I did the math, the timing worked. I mean–" this time it was Mr. Hawk's turn to stutter, "it lined up to, you know, the beach."

Julienne sat back in the chair. She had sat here so many times as a kid sipping on a juice box after she and Daniel had been riding bikes. She had looked up to Mr. Hawk then and she still did now. A million thoughts were in her head all at once, but all she could say was, "Are you mad?"

Mr. Hawk took his time and then shook his head no.

"Why not?"

Mr. Hawk shrugged. Julienne waited.

"Losing Daniel broke my heart," Mr. Hawk leaned forward. "And, that beautiful baby boy, well, he helped."

Julienne sat still.

"He has our name. We're a part of his life. How could I be mad at that?"

Julienne just shook her head.

"You are his grandfather."

"I know."

"Why didn't you say something before?"

"What for?" Mr. Hawk countered. "What good would it have done? You and Greg had reached some type of agreement. Hawk was being raised in a good home. Why would I interfere?"

Julienne looked down.

"Why is this coming up now?"

Julienne's eyes grew filled with tears. She whispered: Greg.

Mr. Hawk stared at her and then the muscles in his face slumped, and he looked very old.

"You mean, on no, Jules, Greg thought..."

"I don't know what Greg thought," Julienne interjected. "We never talked about it. And then in the hospital, he said Hawk looked like Daniel and now, well, now I just don't know."

Mr. Hawk sat back. "This isn't good Jules. I always thought, well, I always thought Greg knew."

Julienne sighed and did her best to explain.

"Daniel died and I thought I was sad from grief. And then I was pregnant, and Greg had wanted another child. He was so happy and I was so sad. I just let him be happy. It was wrong. I never thought ahead. I never considered this."

"Does Camille..."

Julienne shook her head no, saying, "This is a mess."

Julienne just stared at her hands in her lap. It reminded her of the last time she had sat with Daniel at a Waffle House. Things had been a mess then, too.

Julienne took a breath and then looked up. She met Mr. Hawk's gaze. In a whisper she asked, "Do you hate me?"

He shook his head no.

"You were my son's best friend. You gave me a grandson. I'm not the one who will hate you."

Julienne nodded her head and then got up and left.

A week had passed and still no Greg. He was talking to the kids but not Julienne. It was another school night and Julienne was in bed reading *Wuthering Heights* when Camille wandered in with her own book and got in bed with her mom.

Julienne smiled and kept reading. This reminded her of bedtime stories in reverse. Camille was tackling *The Awakening* by Kate Chopin for her AP Language class. Julienne appreciated the novel but she had not shared that with her daughter; she was waiting to hear Camille's opinion.

A few moments passed and Julienne could feel Camille shift in the bed. When she looked over Camille was on her side facing her mother. Camille's book was closed. Julienne wondered if she was sleepy, but her big, brown eyes were wide and focused on her mom.

"So," Camille stated, breaking the silence.

Julienne put her novel down and replied, "So, what?"

"Are we going to talk about this?"

"Talk about what?" Julienne asked as she rolled over on her side to face her daughter.

"Don't be obtuse."

"SAT word," Julienne countered.

"Mother," Camille countered with a roll of the eyes to underscore her exasperation.

"Daughter," Julienne replied in her even schoolteacher

voice.

Camille let out an audible sigh and then said, "Talk about Dad."

"What about him?"

"He hasn't been here in a week."

"You know how he travels for work," even as Julienne said it, she knew the response was weak.

"Except he's not traveling."

"Of course, he is," Julienne answered. She in reality had no idea but she also assumed that was the reason he had given the kids for his absence.

"No, he's not, Mom," and then Camille added, "He is just not sleeping here."

"Well little miss information, where is he sleeping?"

"The Houstonian."

"Oh," Julienne said in a quiet voice.

The Houstonian was no joke. Greg's firm had a membership to the club and she guessed it was easy for him to get a room there. The first time Hawk was old enough to be left alone for a night, Camille's aunt and uncle had babysat the kids and Greg had surprised her with a staycation there. She had a massage and a facial and then they had dinner. What she remembered most was sleeping in and room service for breakfast. She had been grateful to Greg for planning the overnight getaway. That was nine years ago. They had never been back.

"So, are we going to talk about it?"

Julienne sat up in the bed and Camille did the same. For some reason it bothered her that Greg was staying in a nice place. She envisioned him sleeping on the sofa at his office or getting some cheap rate on a weekly rental. Instead, he was staying in the heart of the city in luxe accommodations.

Julienne knew she had hurt Greg, and in her mind the emotional should match the physical and the Houstonian with its mahogany floors, marble countertops, and exclusive membership did not.

Julienne shook her head at herself and refocused. She grabbed her daughter's hand but kept her eyes on the paisley swirls of the duvet cover.

Julienne took a breath and squeezed Camille's hand and stated, "Daniel is Hawk's father."

Moments passed.

Now it was Camille's turn to say "oh," in a quiet voice.

Julienne looked up and Camille continued to stare back at her. Her face was hard to read. Her eyes were wide and her lips pursed. She shifted to cross her legs Indian style.

"Thanks for just going there and telling me, but you are going to have to explain further," Camille said.

For so long Julienne never allowed herself to think about that one week at the beach, but for the second time in a week she remembered and this time she told her daughter.

Camille, to her credit, listened. Julienne did not share every detail; some moments were too sweet and some were too hard and some were just for her and Daniel. She gave her the high points-picking Daniel up from jail, taking the week at the beach, which was meant for him but in the end was also for her.

"And that was in June?"

Julienned nodded.

"And I was with Aunt and Uncle?"

Julienne nodded.

"And Daniel died in August."

Julienne nodded.

"And along came Hawk."

More nodding.

"And Dad never knew."

Another nod.

"Until now."

"Until now," Julienne parroted.

"Why now?"

Julienne shrugged.

"What changed?"

Julienne had no answer.

"Did something happen in the hospital?"

Julienne answered, "He just came in one day and said he looks just like Daniel."

"Well, that's not new."

"What do you mean?"

"He has always looked like Daniel, so why now?"

Julienne had no answer.

"Were you going to leave Dad back then?"

Julienne looked down.

"You weren't sure, were you?"

Julienne looked up and shook her head.

"And then Daniel died," Camille continued to think out loud. "You always said you were best friends."

"We were."

"But he loved you."

"And I loved him, but–"

"No," Camille interjected, "he loved you, mom. Look at that painting. That's not like I love ice cream or I love my dog, that's L-O-V-E, love."

Julienne had no answer. Daniel had said almost the same thing to her way back when.

"Was that one week at the beach like your awakening?" Camille asked, pointing to the cover of her novel.

Julienne took a breath. "I don't know. I never thought of it that way." Silence ensued. "Is that what made you come in here?

Camille nodded. "I just wondered if, like Edna, you had this moment, and I think it was the beach."

Julienne thought it was an interesting theory, and if Camille were her student in her class, she would continue to ask questions and explore the idea, but this was her daughter and her life so she just left the idea alone for now.

"Do you love Dad?"

Julienne nodded.

"But you loved Daniel?"

Julienned nodded.

"Thanks for telling me, Mom."

"Why aren't you more upset? You can be mad," Julienne offered.

"Oh, it's a lot to process. I am sure I will have more questions."

Then Camille added, "I mean, it's kind of a relief, actually."

"What do you mean?"

"Mom, you aren't perfect," Camille said with a curve of her lips, an almost smile.

"Since when was I perfect?"

"My whole life," Camille said. "You do everything just so. The perfect wife, mom, teacher. You are hard to live up to, the girl who should be so screwed up because her parents died when she was a little girl but instead is a model citizen."

"Really? That's how people think of me?"

This time it was Camille's turn to nod.

Julienne leaned back into the tufted headboard and just sat with that perception of herself for a moment.

Camille broke the silence, "But it turns out you are just as screwed up as the next guy. You love two people and one of them is dead."

Camille grinned at her mother.

"Camille Rayne, this is not funny. Are you making jokes?"

"What's the alternative? We sit here and cry?"

Julienne had no answer, and the moment passed.

"Does Hawk know?"

Julienned shook her head. "And don't..."

"I wouldn't," Camille interjected.

More silence.

"Are you and Dad getting a divorce?"

"I don't know. For now, he is not talking to me."

"Wow."

"Yep."

"I miss him, too," Camille stated.

"Dad?" Julienne asked with concern. Greg was talking to the kids. She didn't like hearing this.

"No, Mom," Camille corrected her. "I miss Daniel."

Julienne nodded. This made more sense.

"He adored you," Julienne added. "He loved being your godfather. Don't forget he is the main contributor to your college fund."

"I know, Mom," Camille confirmed. She had heard the story a million times. Daniel's will left everything to his goddaughter, Camille Rayne Eversole. He did not have very much, though. His brother, David, asked for his truck.

The estate sale paid off some outstanding bills. They made some money off the sale of his house and that went into her college fund.

"You always do that," Camille commented.

"Do what?"

"Make sure we know he was so great."

"Well..."

"Well, he wasn't perfect," Camille interrupted.

"I guess that is just what you do when someone dies," Julienne said, almost more to herself. "You remember them in the best light."

"I know he showed up to my birthday party drunk," Camille offered.

"You do," Julienne said more as a question. "You remember that?"

"I remember him dancing with me and spending the night and being sad the next day when he left. Auntie told me the rest and it made sense with what I remember."

Julienne took a breath.

"And he was in trouble when he died."

"Yes, he was dealing with a DUI. I told you that; it's why I took him to the beach."

"And there was the girl."

Julienne's eyes grew big. Julienne tried never to think about that. It was too awful and nothing could be done about it.

"Did Auntie tell you that as well?"

Camille shook her head. "No, Mom, it's called Google. Do you think..."

Now Julienne shook her head. "No, Camille. No, I don't. She had just come forward when Daniel died and none of us knew about it until after the funeral. It just about killed Mr. Hawk. There was no evidence to corroborate her story."

"But..."

Julienne interrupted. "Yes, they were both there that night. Witnesses and bar receipts prove they took turns buying rounds. She left much earlier in the evening. When Daniel was arrested, he was sleeping alone in his truck."

"This isn't me glossing over his shortcomings," Julienne continued to explain. "It's no secret after Daniel's divorce he, well, he went through a lot of women."

Camille once again listened.

"Do I think they had sex that night?" Julienne asked out loud.

"Yes, they probably did, but–" Julienne took a breath. "Do I think for a second, he raped that girl? No, no I don't. He never had problems picking up women; he certainly did not have to force himself on someone. He had faults, but, no, he did not rape her."

Camille just squeezed her mom's hand.

"What else did Google tell you?" Julienne asked, attempting a joke. "Or your aunt?"

Camille did not answer. She reached for her book.

"You know you can talk to me," Julienne said. "You don't have to go to other sources. You can just ask me."

Camille stared at her mom for a moment and said, "I know that, now."

Julienne just nodded.

Camille gave her mom a hug, and Julienne held on tight.

When Camille let go, Julienne gave her a forehead kiss. "Sleep here tonight?"

Camille shook her head. "Think I will head back to my

room. I still have lots of reading to do; plus, you gave me a lot to think about."

"Okay."

Camille started to walk out of the room and then turned, "For me, nothing really changes."

Julienne waited for her to continue.

"You are still my mom. Dad is still my dad. Hawk is still my brother. But for all of you, everything could change."

Camille took three more steps and turned back and asked, "Even though Edna's awakened, she won't get a happy ending, will she?"

Julienne cocked her head as her daughter continued to impress her with her insights.

"Just keep reading."

"Well, she may not get a happy ending, but she deserves one, and so do you, Mom."

With that, Camille walked out. Julienne lay back down. Sleep never came. The conversation with Camille just kept replaying over and over in her head.

CHAPTER 15

Julienne stood in front of Greg's desk. Greg continued to be interested in whatever was on his computer. Julienne felt like she was waiting out a petulant child, but wait she would. His silence had gone on long enough. He had started this conversation in the hospital and now they needed to finish it.

Julienne had come to Greg's office right after school. Greg's secretary had exclaimed in a voice too high, "Julienne, what a surprise."

Julienne had just smiled and kept walking into Greg's office. Greg, to his credit, glanced up from the computer screen, nodded at Julienne, and then went right back to typing.

"Greg, we need..."

"Shut the door," Greg said in a whisper without looking up.

"What?"

"I said," Greg answered in a louder voice, "shut the door."

Julienne did as she was told and then went back to

sitting in front of his desk.

"Sit down."

Julienne chose a seat. Barking out orders was better than Greg not speaking to her.

"Give me three minutes."

Julienne sat back. His office matched his style. Light grey walls with dark wood furniture. A deep blue tufted leather chair Julienne had found for him served as his office chair. On the bookshelves in silver frames were pictures of Camille and Hawk. There was one of them from their wedding. They were holding hands, coming out of the reception, headed to the car. They were smiling.

Greg took five minutes not three, but then he shifted in his chair and made full eye contact with Julienne.

"Well?"

"Well, we need to talk."

"Do we?"

"Yes"

"Why?"

"Because we are married; because we are a family."

Greg remained impassive.

"You started this at the hospital."

Shaking his head, Greg said, "No, Julienne, I did not start this. This, whatever this is, this is all you."

Greg stood up and said, "I really can't talk about this here. You really shouldn't come to my work."

"What else am I supposed to do? You won't answer my calls, my texts. You won't come home. So, I'm here."

"Give me an hour."

"Meet at Lucky's," Greg added.

Julienne wasn't sure about this. Greg could just be trying to get rid of her. She could end up sitting by herself at the bar. He was at least giving her an option, so she took it and nodded her head. Then she grabbed her purse and walked out.

She did not feel like moving her car, so she walked the five blocks to Lucky's, taking in downtown. When they were engaged and first married, Julienne used to meet Greg downtown all the time. Then they had Camille; well, then life happened.

You could see a little bit of everything in downtown. It was mainly corporate but you also had the museums, the churches, and then the trendy places that popped up and then went away as trends went. Then there were places like Lucky's that had always been here to serve downtown. It was not too fancy or too casual. It was like Goldilocks looking for a bed. The bar was just right with seating both in and outside with a wraparound bar, decent food, and a great beer selection. Lucky's was a Houston tradition.

When she got to the bar, she grabbed a table in the back and ordered a beer. She drained that one out of a combination of nerves and thirst. Julienne had just taken a sip of her second beer when Greg walked in, loosening his tie and scanning the bar.

She started to wave or even stand up but she did neither. Instead, she kept sipping her beer and watched her husband of 18 years. His hair was long. She liked it longer; he would want to get it cut. He looked tired. You could see it around his eyes.

He went to the bar and got a beer and then he spotted her. He walked to the table, taking his time with slow, measured steps.

"Thank you for..."

"Were you fucking him the whole time?" Greg

practically spat out the words.

Julienne tilted her head. Her first instinct was to get up and leave but she had insisted they finish this conversation. Greg sat down.

She shook her head no.

"I'm not sure I believe you."

"Greg," she reached out her hand. He grabbed his beer. "You know me. You know us. You know what our family means to me."

He continued to sit there.

"No, Greg, I wasn't fucking him the whole time," Julienne said, answering the question outright while withdrawing her hand.

"Has everyone known the whole time?"

Julienne shook her head no.

"Who do you mean by everyone?"

Greg sat back in his chair and answered, "Your aunt and uncle, Mr. Hawk, your principal, your ob-gyn, everyone."

"No one knew until now."

"What does that mean?"

"I told Mr. Hawk," Julienne looking down.

"And?" Greg asked and waited.

"Camille," Julienne said, still looking down.

"Julienne, god dammit," Greg said between gritted teeth.

"What?" Julienne asked, putting her hands palms up on the table. "You haven't been home in almost two weeks. She asked. I told her."

Greg took a breath and then another sip of beer. "You keep this to yourself for all these years and now you are telling anyone who asks."

Julienne started to say something but then Greg asked, “Were you ever going to tell me?”

Julienne shrugged.

“What does that mean?”

Now it was Julienne’s turn to take a sip. “I, I don’t know. I didn’t plan any of this.”

“He is ten years old,” Greg stated. “Julienne, you have had ten years to figure this out. You didn’t plan this; you plan everything. You planned on cheating on me; you planned on making a fool out of me.”

“No, Greg, no,” Julienne declared, her voice getting louder on each no. She grabbed his hand.

“NO,” she looked into his eyes. “I did not plan the beach. And then he died and then I was pregnant. And our family continued. I did not plan any of this for me or for you, but look what we have. Look at our daughter and our son.”

Greg took his hand back.

He took another sip of beer.

“Except he is not mine,” Greg said again in a quiet voice.

“Yes, yes, he is Greg. You are his dad. You are raising him.”

“Only because Daniel is dead,” Greg said, hanging his head down.

Julienne wanted to get up and go to him, to hug him, to offer comfort in some way. She had caused this pain and now she did not know what to do except be honest in this moment.

“Yes,” Julienne agreed. “Daniel is dead.”

“And if Daniel was alive?”

“It doesn’t matter.”

"Yes, it does," Greg countered.

"No, it doesn't because he is not. Death is final. There are no ifs with death."

"I can't believe you did this."

Before Julienne could answer he asked, "Were you that unhappy?"

Julienne took a breath and he kept going, "Are you even sorry?"

"Did you ever love me?"

"I can't compete with a ghost. I don't think I can do this."

Julienne just sat and took each question–which was really so much more than a question–but when he said this, she snapped back, "Do what?"

She continued, "Have a drink with me? Talk to me? Stay married to me?"

It was her turn to ask questions. Greg hid behind his beer.

Julienne leaned forward. "I have always been so good."

"Excuse me," Greg said his eyebrows rising in question.

"It's exhausting," Julienne said on an exhale. "Since my parents died, I have always been so good. Like if I were good enough nothing bad like that would ever happen again."

Julienne grabbed her beer as if to drink and then thought better of it.

"I am a good wife. I am a good mother. I am a good teacher. I always do what is expected of me. Just once; just one time I let go. I took my best friend to the beach and god help me, I was not a good girl, but don't ask me to be sorry for what happened because that would mean being sorry for Hawk and I won't. I won't be sorry that we have that sweet boy; I won't be sorry for that."

"I love you and I know you probably don't believe me, but I do. And you, you probably hate me right now and while that sucks for me, I understand."

Julienne continued, "You are right; I've known for ten years but it's something I tucked away within myself, I tucked it away with the loss of my friend.

Daniel was dead. I was sad. Then I was pregnant and that, that made everyone–you, Camille, everyone–happy, so that second child I was afraid to have, well, we had him and our life has been good.

So, hate me, yell at me, do what you need to do, Greg," Julienne finished, and then she took a sip of beer.

"I don't know what I need right now," Greg admitted.

They sat there. The bar was filling up with the after-work crowd. All Julienne could hear was chatter. Meanwhile, their conversation had no idle chatter.

"Let's start with something simple. Do you need another beer?"

Greg nodded yes.

Julienne went to the bar and came back with two more.

They sat and they drank. In class Julienne would call this processing time for her students. So much to process for Camille, for Greg, for her.

The waiter put down nachos with jalapenos on the side. Greg started to protest but Julienne interjected and thanked the waiter.

After he walked away, Julienne said, "You also need to eat."

Greg's mouth began to curve. It was almost a smile, but then he caught himself.

They continued to drink. They ate. They talked about Camille and what colleges she should visit in the summer.

Then Greg shifted in his seat and said, "I told Hawk I would pick him up in the morning, go do guy stuff."

Julienne nodded, "Sure."

"Have you told him?"

"No," Julienne started to say more but left it at that.

"Are you going to tell him?"

"No."

"Did you ever plan to tell him?"

Julienne said, "I told you, Greg. I did not plan this. Telling him would mean telling you, and no, I had no plan."

"Please don't tell him anything, yet."

"I won't."

"Not until we figure this out."

Greg put some money on the table and got up to leave.

Julienne struggled to come up with something to say that would compel Greg to stay. Without thinking she asked, "Why now?"

Greg jerked his head up from the money and said, "Excuse me?"

"Why now?" Julienne repeated. "Hawk has always looked like Daniel, so why now? Why bring it up at the hospital. You say I have had ten years to figure this out, but for ten years you loved your son who looked like my neighbor."

Greg maintained eye contact. Julienne waited.

A moment passed and he shrugged his shoulders and said, "Blood type."

Julienne cocked her head and considered this answer.

"The nurse was holding the tablet reviewing Hawk's

chart out loud and as she went through his list of information, she said his blood type."

Greg sighed. "It just hit me then. He does not have my blood type. And he does not have yours. Then Google told me the rest."

Julienne just shook her head. Google had been providing her family lots of information lately.

Julienne started to say something, but Greg shook his head.

"I will see you in the morning when I pick up Hawk."

Greg took two steps and turned around to ask, "It only happened at the beach?"

Looking in his eyes she could see how hard it was for him to ask this. She bit her lip and then said in almost a whisper, "Yes, only at the beach."

Greg blinked and then walked off.

Julienne leaned back in her chair and then drank what was left of her beer while she once again replayed yet another difficult conversation with someone she loved.

CHAPTER 17

August 2010

Two years had passed since Daniel's death and not a day went by when Julienne didn't think of her neighbor. The painting of her was now encased in a chunky ornate dark wood frame and hung in the foyer. Greg had chosen the frame and the spot. He said he wanted everyone who came to their house to see it, to see his wife.

Today Julienne was doing much the same thing she had when she got the news of Daniel's death. She was sitting on the back porch watching her children play. Gaston the rescue pup was still ruling over the backyard, running between the kids and also coming to Julienne with his tail wagging in need of a pat on the head.

She should go inside and start dinner. Greg would be home soon and the meat was defrosted, but Hawk was too cute pushing his toy lawn mower and Camille wanted her mother to see every trick she attempted on the trampoline, so Julienne continued to sit just a moment longer. The lawn mower spewed bubbles in the air which Gaston tried in vain to catch.

Julienne's phone was providing background music.

She had put it on shuffle play so any random song from her library could come up and they almost all contained a memory.

The next song up was Ray Lamontagne's "Let It Be Me." While she would never take this song off her playlist, since losing Daniel she never listened to it either. However, today Julienne leaned back in her chair and thought of the first time she played that song for Daniel.

It was August 1993, right before she was to leave for college. Julienne would normally skip that song, but today she took a breath and allowed herself to relive that afternoon.

"Daniel, do me a favor?" Julienne had asked.

Daniel had been boxing up Julienne's shoes which she would be taking with her to Sam Houston. One lock of dark blond hair fell in his left eye when he looked up to answer her question. He had on a white V-neck shirt and a worn-out pair of jeans. Today his eyes appeared to be a light shade of brown. He was helping Julienne pack up for the fall. Tomorrow she was headed to Sam Houston University. She was both excited and nervous. It would be a big change for her to be away from her aunt and uncle–and especially Daniel.

Daniel was taking classes at Houston Community College, and he had a job working construction. They would be about an hour away from each other–which might as well be about ten hours apart, considering the access she had possessed the last ten years.

"Aren't I already?" Daniel questioned back.

Julienne hesitated. In her hesitation, she bit her bottom lip. She wanted him, needed him, to say yes.

She pushed back a wisp of hair that had escaped from

her ponytail.

"Jules," Daniel continued, standing up straight from being hunched over the box. "I'm helping you pack. Isn't that already a favor?"

Julienne grinned. She walked over to him. Her ponytail swung back and forth across her shoulders as she walked. She was wearing cut-off shorts and an orange Sam Houston tank. She looked down at her bare feet with her toes freshly painted in a hue of tangerine and took a breath. Then she tugged on the hem of his shirt as she looked up at him.

"This," she said, "is a different kind of favor."

Daniel didn't move. He also didn't answer. They just stood there close but not touching, except for her hand still holding on to his shirt. He never broke eye contact but waited on her to elaborate.

Julienne bit her bottom lip again and then said it in a hurry before she lost her nerve, "Have sex with me."

Daniel's eyes went wide. Then he smiled. Julienne had not been sure what his response would be, but a smile was a hopeful sign.

Then Daniel began to laugh, more like a chuckle, but that was not the response Julienne wanted.

She let go of his shirt and took a step back, folding her arms across her chest.

"That's funny, Jules," Daniel said, turning back to the box he was taping up.

"I wasn't joking," Julienne said, looking down at her tangerine toes. She continued to stand with her arms folded.

Daniel looked over his shoulder.

"What?" he asked.

"I wasn't joking," she repeated louder this time with more conviction.

Daniel turned back to face her.

"Well, you can't be serious," he said.

"Why not?" she asked.

Daniel started pacing. Julienne stood still.

"Because," Daniel said, running his fingers through his hair. "I mean, there's so many reasons."

"Like," Julienne prodded.

"Well, for starters, you never have before."

"Exactly," Julienne said. "So, I don't want to go off to college a virgin. I am so tired of this hanging over my head. I just want to be done with it."

Daniel was shaking his head.

"Not like this, Jules. You should wait..."

"Until it's special, until I'm in love," Julienne finished for him, rolling her eyes as she said it. "Don't patronize me."

"Jules, your first time should be," he paused, "it just shouldn't be like this, not in the middle of the day with your neighbor."

"I disagree," Julienne countered. "This is exactly how it should be. I trust you and you know what you are doing. There doesn't have to be any big build-up, just my friend showing me how it's done."

Daniel shook his head.

"At least let me think about it. Let me plan something. I can get us a hotel room or..."

Julienne shook her head.

"Right here, right now."

"But your aunt and uncle," Daniel retorted.

"Gone all day," Julienne said, moving to her door,

closing it, and locking it.

"Jules, this doesn't seem right."

She was walking back to him but paused long enough to change the song that was playing. She put on Ray Lamontagne's "Let It Be Me." She stopped right in front of him.

"Is it me," she asked. "I mean, do I not do anything for you?" she asked her voice cracking just a little.

Daniel took a step closer and touched the left side of her face.

"God, no, Jules. You're beautiful. Any guy would be lucky to be with you."

Julienne stripped off her shirt and slid off her shorts. She stood in front of Daniel in a white lace bra and hip hugger panties while Ray sang:

That's when you need someone
Someone that you can call

"I don't want any guy," she said, pulling out her ponytail. Her dark hair hung straight down her back. "I want you."

Daniel took a visible breath and stepped closer. They were inches apart. He put his hands on either side of her face. His touch felt safe.

"Jules, are you sure?" he asked, looking down into her eyes.

She put her hands on his hips. Every nerve in her body tingled from anticipation. She nodded her head yes.

Daniel leaned down and for a moment she thought she was going to get the usual forehead kiss, but instead he brushed his lips softly across hers.

He paused to see her reaction. She smiled. He kissed her again, this time longer. She melted into him. One hand grabbed the back of his hair. The other went around to his back. She moaned when his tongue found hers. He picked her up and she wrapped her legs around his waist. He led them to the bed and laid her down.

"Jules," Daniel said, standing beside the bed.

"Don't talk," she pleaded, reaching for a belt loop. "Just keep going."

Daniel took off his shirt. Then he unbuttoned his jeans and slid those off as well. He stood in his boxers and she could see he was aroused and this made her grin.

Daniel got on all fours on top of her. He brushed her hair back on the right side of her face and then kissed her neck. Then he kissed her collar bone. Then he kissed the top of each of her breasts, which made her arch her back. He reached around and unsnapped her bra in one motion. They were chest to chest. His body was warm and hard; Julienne reveled in the weight of him on top of her.

The rest was a delicious blur for Julienne. His hands and mouth were everywhere and her body delighted in all of it. He took his time and just when she thought she was about to explode, he entered her. She inhaled a sharp breath. It both hurt and felt right all at the same time.

Daniel locked eyes with her and stroked slowly. She moved her hips to meet his and their rhythm increased. When she came, she threw her head back and basked in the pure pleasure of the moment. Daniel collapsed on top of her, breathing hard.

"You okay?" he asked.

Julienne nodded her head yes. Then he gave her a forehead kiss. He laid his head on the cushion of her breasts. They drifted off to sleep tangled in each other.

Later, when Julienne woke, her room was darker. She was lying tangled up in her neighbor, surrounded by boxes. This was the beginning and an end for Julienne, and the way they had spent the afternoon was the perfect way to celebrate that.

Julienne stretched out one leg and then eased herself out from under Daniel. He kept sleeping. She cleaned up in the restroom. Staring at herself in the mirror as she put her hair back up in a ponytail, she did not look any different. Julienne felt different, though. She felt ready to move on to the next chapter in her life.

Julienne went back to packing. Daniel woke up about twenty minutes later. His hair was shooting out in every direction and for a moment he looked like the boy she met on that first day all those years ago. Then he sat up and the covers fell away, and it was clear he was a man.

"Jules," Daniel yawned her name. "What are you doing?"

Julienne grinned, "Packing, silly."

"Smart ass," Daniel replied as he swung his legs over and got out of bed. She busied herself with a box while he dressed. He came up beside her and finished closing the box.

"Jules, do we need to talk about this?"

Julienne shook her head no.

"And we're good?"

Julienne smirked.

"Well, I can't speak for you, but I'm great."

She gave him a good game pat on the butt as she walked out of her room.

"Thirsty," she yelled back. "Getting some water."

Daniel just shook his head.

The next day Julienne left for Sam Houston University. They never spoke about that afternoon. It was almost as if it did not happen, except of course it did. Julienne would always smile when people talked about their first times: awkward, wrong person, awful locale. She would always just shrug and say mine was with some guy in high school, like it was no big deal. The only time she felt bad was when Greg brought up their first times. She gave him the usual vague story and glossed over the details.

Every now and then, though, in a quiet moment she would allow herself to think about it, about how bold and shy she was at the same time, about how she couldn't imagine her first time with anyone other than Daniel, about how it was so mind-blowingly good that the memory of it still made her toes curl, but then she would lock the extraordinary memory back away and go on with her ordinary life.

Her life now included a sweet boy with spiky hair and hazel eyes who liked to blow kisses at his momma as he pushed his lawn mower. If Greg ever wondered, he never said a word. He was, at least on the outside, so happy to have another baby. Sometimes she wondered what that said about her husband. In the end, she remained with Greg, grateful for his loyalty and for being a good father.

Julienne had at first thought her response to the painting was shock and it partially was, but it was also morning sickness, which she actually had morning, noon, and night.

They named him Gregory Hawk Eversole. For Julienne, this honored both her husband and her neighbor.

When she watched her children play, she saw only

mini versions of Julienne and Daniel, except this generation would grow up happier. Camille would never be silent because she lost her parents and Hawk would never be angry because his mother left. Julienne would make sure her Hawk was always loved.

Hawk made a pass by her with the lawn mower and blew her kiss. Her chest tightened. She should tell Greg. She must tell Greg.

She blew a kiss back to Hawk and then reminded herself that should was her least favorite word.

And when she thought of that week at the beach, Julienne knew she should feel guilty but she didn't. She felt grateful for the time with Daniel. She felt grateful that the trip brought her a son. In the end, Daniel may be dead, but the best parts of him lived on in a boy named Hawk.

Then she got up to go inside to make dinner and never thought of telling Greg again.

CHAPTER 18

March 2027

Julienne looked out across the crowd and smiled. The sky was clear. A breeze was blowing. Having Hawk's high school graduation party at the beach had been a good decision.

Next August Hawk would head off to Tulsa University. Following in his father's footsteps had made Greg beyond proud. Of course, Hawk wanted to study architecture. He wanted to create great big beautiful buildings, so in a sense he was following in both his fathers' footsteps.

A blue plastic cup full of beer appeared in front of her. Julienne followed the hand to see Camille was offering the drink to her.

"You need this," said her daughter.

Julienne looked over at her daughter. Her hair was shoulder-length. She had on a blue halter top with cutoff shorts and flip-flops. She looked exactly as she should for a cookout at the beach.

Camille continued to be gracious when told she was like her mother. Camille had just finished her first year of law school. Julienne's greatest accomplishment was raising her two children and doing her best for them to feel loved and safe and secure. Camille might look like her mother but with her passion and ambition, Camille's greatest accomplishment would be changing the world for the better. Of that, Julienne had no doubt.

All of this went through her mind as she took the beer from her daughter.

"Where's the boyfriend?" Julienne asked.

"He's on his way," Camille answered and then added, "He has a name."

Julienne smiled and repeated what her uncle used to say to her back in the day, "I will learn his name when he becomes something more important."

Camille rolled her eyes at her mother. Julienne smiled. Thinking of her uncle made her want to check on her aunt. She found her sitting in a lawn chair with her big floppy hat on to shield the sun. In her mind her aunt was not old, but looking at her now there was no denying it. Aging gracefully still meant aging. Her hair was solid white pulled back in a low ponytail at the nape of her neck. At 89, her eyes were still bright and her smile wide. They were planning a big party for her ninetieth in the fall. She just wished her uncle was still here. They lost him two years ago.

Her aunt was eating and talking to their beach neighbor, the grey cabin guy. He had bought the cabin next door five years ago and the kids teased Julienne because she could never remember his name and always referred to him as the grey cabin guy. Greg had pointed out that she never called people by their names, just labels: neighbor, Aunt, Uncle, grey cabin guy.

Julienne continued to make the rounds. David, Daniel's

brother, was in charge of the grill.

Hawk was surrounded by his friends. Mr. Hawk was holding the door open for Greg, who was bringing out more ice for the coolers.

Everything was done, so Julienne took her beer down to the water. She slipped off her sandals and felt the warmth of the sand and the waves lapping at her feet. She closed her eyes and just breathed.

"Are you thinking of him?"

Julienne opened her eyes at the sound of the voice behind her and shook her head no.

"It's okay if you are," Greg said. "I'm sure..."

"I'm not," Julienne said, looking back to grab his hand so he was standing right beside her. "The beach is wrapped up in so many memories, my parents, our family, yes, Daniel, but he does not own the beach."

Greg just held her hand.

Julienne faced him and said, "And now Hawk's graduation will be tied to the beach."

Greg squeezed her hand.

"So, what were you thinking of?"

Julienne laughed. "It will probably make no sense to you."

"Try me."

"I was thinking of Edna."

"Who?"

"Edna from *The Awakening*. Camille and I have debated about her. Did she deserve a happy ending? She tried but then she gives up or society gives up on her. Either way, it all begins and ends for her at the beach."

"Julienne, you lost me," Greg said, smiling. The wind was blowing his hair, which each year had more grey. His light brown eyes were sparkling in the sun and while she started to tell him he needed his sunglasses; she was also glad to be looking into his eyes.

Julienne looked at Greg. She remembered that day after Lucky's when Greg had picked up Hawk. That night he had offered to pick up Chinese takeout and they had eaten together as a family. A week later he had called and asked about coming home. He stayed in the guest room, but it was a step. She offered to go to therapy, to which he said no and later yes.

One day she came home and the painting was gone. Her heart sank with the idea that he had destroyed it, but she said nothing because she could understand him not wanting that reminder on display. Instead, Greg moved the painting to the beach. The following weekend he took her to the Bayou Arts Festival, where they chose a painting together to go in the foyer. Then instead of going home, they checked into the Houstonian for the night. It was the first time they had slept together since Hawk had been in the hospital.

It was a series of steps, some small, some big that led them back together. Then one day Julienne looked up and she was living, truly living and enjoying life with the man in front of her who loved her.

Julienne brushed his hair back from his eyes. Greg wrapped one arm around the small of her back and leaned in to whisper, "I like you in this red dress."

Julienne grinned and whispered back, "I know."

Greg continued, "Reminds me of being your wedding date."

"And dancing to songs about rain."

"And telling you I love you."

Julienne bit her lip.

And now, just like then, all was as it should be. She had a best friend who she loved fiercely who was dead. She had a husband who loved her and forgave her. She had two beautiful children. She didn't answer Greg with words but instead leaned in for a kiss.

Just then the first notes of "Brown Eyed Girl" could be heard from the party.

Camille shouted, "Mom, come dance."

Greg reluctantly ended the kiss.

"I know the rules," he stated. "When that song plays, my two favorite girls dance."

Julienne smiled.

"Always," Julienne agreed. "Of course, our favorite guy is dancing with us."

Greg smiled wider.

Julienne did not know if she deserved this, but she was determined to embrace the life before her.

Julienne walked with Greg hand in hand back to the party.

EPILOGUE

August 2008

Daniel was in his truck with the windows rolled down and the radio turned up. His truck was loaded with some clothes, some food, but for the most part, art supplies. He was headed to the coast to paint.

It had been two months since his encounter with the law. His DUI had been knocked down to public intoxication since technically he had not been driving his truck, only sleeping in it. Daniel had to pay a fine, complete community service hours, and attend mandatory alcohol education classes.

He had been eating right and trying to live right. He had been spending time at the animal shelter as part of his community service. Cleaning out kennels and walking dogs was good exercise for him. When he looked in the rearview mirror his eyes were clear, not bloodshot.

Today his eyes looked green because he had on a dark green shirt Julienne had given him. She thought he wore too much blue; plus, she always liked it when his eyes looked green. She said it reminded him of her dad.

Daniel's hair was getting long, again something

Julienne preferred. She liked to run her fingers through it and he liked her touch so he let it grow. And he had a day-old beard.

On his way out of town, he had dropped two of his paintings off at a local gallery. The third he had mailed.

The first notes of "Brown Eyed Girl" came over the radio. Without hesitation, Daniel turned up the volume. He started to reach for his phone to text Jules, but he stopped himself. That wasn't the deal they had made. Daniel had made her a promise and he intended to keep it. He resisted the urge to contact her.

Instead, he let the song wash over him as he continued to drive.

Daniel remembered the solemn little girl he had met on that first afternoon with her dark hair pulled back and big brown eyes so scared. He thought back to a college-bound Jules running around in her Sam Houston orange, hair still long with eyes not scared but bold and ready to face the world. Julienne danced across his memory in a red dress in New Orleans with a silver "J" necklace dangling from her neck. The last image was her standing on the deck at the beach with the sunset at her back, her long dark hair swirling around her shoulders, and her big brown eyes smiling at him.

That is the Jules he thought of as he drove down the highway singing along to her favorite song.

ACKNOWLEDGMENTS

Thank you to Nick, Trista, Kyle, and the whole team at Atmosphere Press. Your expertise and collaborative process made this novel a reality. Thank you to my hometown for providing the backdrop to this story. Thank you to my family for your patience and support. Most of all, thank you to my neighbor. On a random night in a hole-in-the-wall bar with Van Morrison playing in the background, you dared me to write a novel inspired by you. Challenge accepted.

ABOUT ATMOSPHERE PRESS

Atmosphere Press is an independent, full-service publisher for excellent books in all genres and for all audiences. Learn more about what we do at atmospherepress.com.

We encourage you to check out some of Atmosphere's latest releases, which are available at Amazon.com and via order from your local bookstore:

Saints and Martyrs: A Novel, by Aaron Roe

When I Am Ashes, a novel by Amber Rose

Melancholy Vision: A Revolution Series Novel, by L.C. Hamilton

The Recoleta Stories, by Bryon Esmond Butler

Voodoo Hideaway, a novel by Vance Cariaga

Hart Street and Main, a novel by Tabitha Sprunger

The Weed Lady, a novel by Shea R. Embry

A Book of Life, a novel by David Ellis

It Was Called a Home, a novel by Brian Nisun

Grace, a novel by Nancy Allen

Shifted, a novel by KristaLyn A. Vetovich

Because the Sky is a Thousand Soft Hurts, stories by Elizabeth Kirschner

ABOUT THE AUTHOR

Photo credit @photography_with_purpose

D. A. Olivier was born and raised in Houston, TX. Growing up she was fascinated with dance and books. Now she channels her creativity through writing. She earned her bachelor's and master's degree at Lamar University. She received her PhD at Oklahoma State University. She currently lives in the Houston area with her family and three rescue dogs. Readers can follow her rescue dogs on Instagram @Olivierdogs. You can follow the author as well @daolivier24.